JAMES WOOD is a book critic at *The New Yorker* and the recipient of a National Magazine Award in criticism. He is the author of several essay collections, the novel *The Book Against God*, and the study *How Fiction Works*. He is a professor of the practice of literary criticism at Harvard University.

ALSO BY JAMES WOOD

FICTION

The Book Against God

NONFICTION

The Nearest Thing to Life

The Fun Stuff: And Other Essays

How Fiction Works

The Irresponsible Self: On Laughter and the Novel

The Broken Estate: Essays on Literature and Belief

Additional Praise for

Upstate

"[A] crisply written comedy . . . both exegesis and hosanna."
—*O, The Oprah Magazine*

"Novels about fathers and their grown daughters are rare, and James Wood's *Upstate* is a welcome addition." —*Vogue*

"*Upstate* is resolutely a novel of character, and the intelligence that animates it is recognizably Wood's . . . Family reconfiguration is *Upstate*'s overt theme, and that is treated with great subtlety and comic grace." —Christian Lorentzen, *Vulture*

"Nearly flawless . . . Everything on the page is seeable and believable, often enlivened by [James Wood's] dry English wit."
—Ann Levin, Associated Press

"Wood can produce sentences as fine as bone china."
—Claire Allfree, *The Daily Mail* (London)

"Uncharted physical and emotional terrain collide in James Wood's thoughtful and thought-provoking second novel, *Upstate*, a deceptively gentle exploration of the wounds of the past, the complex mesh of family relationships, and the ways in which they aid or obstruct our strategies for healing."
—Rebecca Abrams, *Financial Times*

"Upstate has a confident quietness . . . [A] gentle, almost lighthearted realist novel, with a lovely warmth."
—Jonathan McAloon, *The Irish Times*

"A great strength of *Upstate* is its general snap and vigor, and one sees this across Wood's criticism, too."

—Emma Brockes, *The Guardian*

"The writing is beautiful, the location snow-crunchingly real . . . A quietly engrossing read."

—Ella Walker, *The Herald* (Scotland)

"This is how fiction works."   —David Annand, *Literary Review*

"Modest, deeply humane revelations . . . Polished, poignant, and often very funny."

—Hephzibah Anderson, *The Mail on Sunday* (London)

"Wood contemplates deep questions while painting an indelible portrait of a family coming to grips, clarifying complex, recognizable problems as he moves his characters forward in ways that seem real and satisfying. Pitch-perfect and highly recommended."

—Barbara Hoffert, *Library Journal* (starred review)

Upstate

Upstate

JAMES WOOD

Picador
Farrar, Straus and Giroux
New York

UPSTATE. Copyright © 2018 by James Wood. All rights reserved. Printed in the United States of America. For information, address Picador, 175 Fifth Avenue, New York, N.Y. 10010.

picadorusa.com • instagram.com/picador
twitter.com/picadorusa • facebook.com/picadorusa

Picador® is a U.S. registered trademark and is used by Macmillan Publishing Group, LLC, under license from Pan Books Limited.

For book club information, please visit facebook.com/picadorbookclub or email marketing@picadorusa.com.

Designed by Jonathan D. Lippincott

The Library of Congress has cataloged the Farrar, Straus and Giroux edition as follows:

Names: Wood, James, 1965– author.
Title: Upstate / James Wood.
Description: First edition. | New York : Farrar, Straus and Giroux, 2018.
Identifiers: LCCN 2017038336 | ISBN 9780374279530 (hardcover) | ISBN 9780374718206 (ebook)
Subjects: LCSH: Dysfunctional families—Fiction. | Self-realization—Fiction. | Domestic fiction.
Classification: LCC PR6123.O527 U67 2018 | DDC 823'.92—dc23
LC record available at https://lccn.loc.gov/2017038336

Picador Paperback ISBN 978-1-250-21505-5

Our books may be purchased in bulk for promotional, educational, or business use. Please contact your local bookseller or the Macmillan Corporate and Premium Sales Department at 1-800-221-7945, extension 5442, or by email at MacmillanSpecialMarkets@macmillan.com.

First published by Farrar, Straus and Giroux

First Picador Edition: June 2019

D   10   9   8   7   6   5   4   3   2

For Claire, Livia, and Lucian

Upstate

1

First he would have to go and see his mother. He would tell her—something about Vanessa, not everything of course. The home, six miles along a favorite road, was a formidable old place, with that gray strictness of the north he loved. But now it looked abandoned: everything was in wintry abeyance. Four years she had been living there, and he was still never sure how to announce himself. It was also ridiculously expensive, he could no longer afford it. What did she, what did *he*, get for the money? Two small rooms rather than one, extra space for the dark massing of a lifetime's heavy old furniture; and maybe she got two biscuits with her tea on Fridays.

He made his way through two huffing fire doors, which bottled a weekend's stale yeast. School food. Outside his mother's room ("Clarendon"), he gathered himself a bit like a clown, pulling up his trousers, dusting down his coat, and entered with a light knock. The television was off, thank goodness. She was asleep in the chintz chair his father had used as the family throne, issuing directives and decrees from behind his newspaper. She was tiny, sunken, some of her teeth were out. The old music hall joke . . . *Her teeth are like stars. They come out at night.* But it was early afternoon. As she breathed, something seemed to catch in her throat. She'd always had a large nose, and now she seemed to be reducing around it, shrinking down to bone, the nose tenacious,

final, rootlike. I have hers, so this will be mine, right enough. He
knelt beside her, and whispered. She opened her eyes, and said
with slight affront, "When did you get here, Alan?" as if he'd
been spying on her.

"Just a second ago."

"Fetch me my teeth—by the side of the bed, please, in the
glass." She turned away from him to insert the plate. "Now we
need to call for some tea and biscuits. They'll bring it, if you
ask." As a child, in a lower-middle-class suburb of Edinburgh,
she had made herself unpopular at school by affecting an English,
or maybe Anglo-Scots, pronunciation; since his dad's death, her
accent seemed to have moved up the ranks again, by another notch
or two. It usually had the effect of making her sound slightly
irritable.

In truth, these days she sounded like the mistress but looked
more like the servant—short, bent, too modestly or shabbily
dressed today.

"You don't need to wear this shawl thing, do you?" he said,
lifting it over her shoulders.

"Certainly not, I just put it on for my nap. Thank you . . . *You*
look very tired. You know you can't burn your candle at both ends."

"A Roman candle, maybe?" He had just had his sixty-eighth
birthday. "How are you?"

"All right, I suppose . . . but this English view isn't my landscape, of course," she added, gesturing at the window with splendid
authority.

"Well, it's not a bad one," he said, looking at the line of leaf-
less trees, and the icy hills. He was paying for that English view.
"And we've been over this. You don't want to live with me, you
need your independence, though it would be a lot cheaper if you
did move in with us."

"Absolutely not. I took in your grandmother, as you perfectly
well know, and it made my fifties a complete *blank*. All I did, day
after day, was look after her. I'll never do that to you."

In that house, the two women had seemed to detest each other; with stealthy expertise, each made the other immovably depressed.

"But you want me to visit. And I want to visit you." He took her hand. "You're no good to me three hours away up in Scotland, even though you'd have your *own landscape* there." He said it gently.

The tea arrived, carried by a very red teenage boy. He offered a biscuit to both of them, and then left, making sure to take the full plate with him.

"Wartime rations round here!" said his mother. The young man appeared again.

"Mrs. Querry," he said, "I'm supposed to remind you that the residents are gathering at three-thirty in the sun lounge for the winter flu vaccination. It's, you know, the booster for them that missed it first time round. Need any help?"

"No, I have my son. Thank you."

The room could have been a lot worse. High ceilings with ornate moldings, Roman laurels almost; textured wallpaper with chips in it like slivered almonds—though in fact these always made him think of splinters caught under a child's skin—all painted a pleasant cream. And parental things he had known all his life: a watercolor reproduction of Durham Cathedral, an antique mirror that you couldn't really see yourself in (it looked valuable but he knew it wasn't), a cushion whose faded lilac cover, bought by him at Heal's, London, on the Tottenham Court Road, had not been replaced in thirty years at least. It was all pretty good, or as good as can be when one's whole life has been reduced to souvenirs of selfhood. It was a nice place. But he couldn't afford it any longer.

She looked at him with her pale blue eyes: Vanessa's.

"This whole place is up in arms! My next-door neighbor lost her hearing aid yesterday, she put it in some tissue paper on her bedside table and the cleaner threw it out by mistake, she thought it was a bit of rubbish. And in the room that's just two doors down the hall, Mary Binet is furious because she likes to talk French to another woman here who can understand it, she's the only woman who can, and now Mary's been told to stop talking French by the staff—apparently, someone else, we all assume it's one of the residents and I have a very good idea *who*, has complained that they're speaking a *secret language* to exclude everyone else. I'll miss it, I couldn't understand what they were saying, but I liked hearing the French . . . And now the manager is leaving at the end of the month, she's only been here for six months, she's Czech I think, a nice woman though for some reason she *hates* to be thought of as Polish—"

He interrupted her. "Ma, I have to go to America for a week."

"America? Well, well. On business?" She had always enjoyed enunciating those words, so he spoke them back to her, with finality:

"On business."

"Well, don't . . . get caught up in anything."

"Caught up in anything?"

"It's a dangerous place, from what I hear . . . There was that terrible thing with the towers. You'll go and see Vanessa? She's always wanted you to visit her in . . . in that place . . ."

"In Saratoga Springs."

"Yes, I wanted to say . . . Sarsaparilla."

"I will see her. And Josh."

"Oh good lord . . . courage, there! He's far too young, and certainly not good enough for her—"

"You've never even met him!"

"Yes, that's two of us, but I do have a telephone here, you know, I get *reports*, and I was about to say—before you interrupted me—that Vanessa isn't getting any younger, is she?"

"Ma, I can't keep up with you—now you're giving him your blessing?"

"Well why shouldn't the poor thing have a boyfriend? Maybe

Josh is the one? And when they marry, *you'll* blame him for taking Vanessa away . . ."

"Oh, Vanessa was already away. Well away. She did her Ph.D. there, not here, after all. That was the beginning."

"Silly girl. It was a shame she didn't come back at Christmas. I suppose she'd rather spend time with her beau." There was a moment or two of old-fashioned silence: the tick of his mother's fancy carriage clock. His gift.

"Alan love, can you help me to the sunroom? I want to get there early—while the needle is still sharp . . ."

They smiled at each other, and he helped her up and went beside her as she gripped the mouse-gray tubular walker, a marvel of engineering, as strong as a weight lifter but as light as the bones of a very old lady, with wheels on the front and two splayed yellow tennis balls stuck on the back legs. These dragged along the carpet as the aged couple, mother and son, moved slowly down the corridor.

2

The House of Querry certainly looked good—as if it were built on rock rather than sand. A curved gravel path (as he drove up it now, his car tires ground and displaced the little blanched pebbles in an expensive flurry), ample stones, tall windows, a black metal "S" to keep some sagging stonework together, a stout old front door, a bent black iron boot scraper (the kind you could never buy, only inherit). It was circa 1860. Alan Querry hadn't built it, but sometimes felt as if he had. Here he and Cathy had brought up Vanessa and Helen, and here he had raised them, after Cathy walked out. Here was the window he'd replaced, on his own, there the guttering he'd fixed, on his own, there the garage roof he'd replaced with the help of Rob, the slightly retarded odd-job man from the village.

It looked like the place of someone who'd done well for himself. He lived in the poshest part of Northumberland, where all the neighbors, if that was the word for people so richly distant, seemed to be "gentleman farmers." They had all boarded at Eton, and strode around the county wearing those rust-colored baggy corduroys, tired but glowing somehow like the embers of old money. (Where did they get those "old" but very expensive new clothes? New & Lingwood, Jermyn Street, London: he'd once shopped there himself, triumphant but sweaty in the hushed emporium.) His nearest neighbor was a balding, middle-aged bar-

onet, a gentle but unremarkable chap who had done nothing at
all in his life, and whose only distinction, celebrated in the area,
was that he read *The Shining* when it was first published, and was
so scared he'd been unable to sleep for three whole days and
nights.

It wasn't Alan's world. His father left school at sixteen and
went into the shipbuilding industry in Newcastle. Da was clever
and industrious, and was soon working at Parsons, buying parts
for their great steam turbines. Alan was born in Newcastle; after
the war, the Querry family moved to Durham, and Da eventually
opened a big hardware shop there—on Saddler Street, on the
way up to the cathedral. His father had truly established himself;
not just a "shopkeeper" but a "proprietor," whose name was pro-
verbial in town: "*I'm popping into Querry's.*" Da never made more
of it than that, though. It was seeing his father try and fail to ex-
pand, try and fail to acquire a second shop, that gave Alan the idea
of going into property—first in Durham, then in Newcastle,
York, Manchester. Their only child liked making enough money
of his own to buy his parents a brand-new Volvo—the only new
car they ever owned—and to pay his dad's hospice bills, when the
end came.

Now he was paying his mum's bills, and he couldn't afford it,
and no one, least of all Helen and Vanessa, would believe him
when he told them this, it would be incomprehensible to them.
How could the Querry Property Group, with buildings through-
out the north of England, even a shiny (but it was only one-room!)
new office in Manchester and a fancy website designed by an
American firm from Salt Lake City—how could all that not keep
on paying and paying?

He walked across the gravel and pushed open the heavy front
door. Otter jumped from his basket, writhing with pleasure. He
hadn't seen Candace's car at the front, so perhaps she was out.
There was no one in the kitchen, nor in the expensively subdued
sitting room. The French windows glowed; the short February

afternoon was sloping away. It was very still. For so many years, after Cathy left, and after the children went off to university, the house had seemed desperately quiet; the thick carpet held the ghost of their footsteps. He even thought about selling the beautiful old place. Candace had changed all that. His daughters, Helen especially, didn't much like her. Among other things, they found her free-market anticommunism strident. Well, *he* didn't like Candace's politics that much; he'd always been reflexively Labour, everyone in Durham was, even the successful ones who "got away." Maybe they were jealous, as they got older and grayer and wider—as they *wanned* (Vanessa's coinage, combining "wane" and "wan")—jealous of her still-black hair, straight and glossy, her trim hips, her formidable vitality. The only time he'd seriously attempted to get his daughters together with Candace, they argued about whether Mrs. Thatcher had been "a net benefit" to the country (Candace's brisk conclusion) or a bloody disaster (Helen's). Vanessa later said she found Candace "coercive"; Van had sulked like a child and retreated to her bedroom, he now recalled.

Whatever Vanessa and Helen felt about the situation, he'd been saved by Candace, that he was sure about. She was ten years younger than him, and had great optimism and strength. She had saved him from solitude, from overwork and the widower's musty celibacy, saved him from aging, from dying, even.

"Candace! . . . Candace, love?"

She was in the small television room at the back of the house, sitting cross-legged on a dense round cushion. For over a decade, Candace had been a management consultant in Hong Kong, but she told Alan she had never liked it much. A year ago she decided to train to become a Buddhist psychotherapist. There was an emphasis on meditation, of course—and gardens, somehow. The self like a plant, perhaps—growing, dying, reborn. She now spent a fair amount of time sitting on that low cushion, which was covered in crimson chinoiserie, and he knew it was coarse of him but she always seemed to be basically *asleep*, not meditating. Helen said that Candace lacked any obvious therapeutic gifts. ("It's like Quincy Jones attempting monogamy.") Alan laughed willingly, and later looked up "Quincy Jones" on Google. It wasn't true, not at least about Candace Lee.

She was intense, dry, coherent: she could do no wrong. Alan saw that she was shoeless—her naked feet.

"Did you tell her?" Candace disliked his mother, was amusingly bad at hiding it.

"Well, I told her I had to go to America."

"Of course I don't mean that, Alan. You didn't tell her *why* you're going there?" She got up from the floor, as if it was easy.

"I don't think this is the right moment," he said. "I'll wait till I've come back."

"You were afraid."

"I suppose I am, a bit."

She drew closer and lightly tapped his chest.

"You can't be afraid, you have to be *there* for Vanessa. She needs you."

"Be there for her . . ."

"Yes, you have to be there for her, I'm not embarrassed by that phrase. You are her father, so you must embody what it means to go on, why you go on doing what you do."

"I 'go on,' I suppose, because I don't think about life too much."

"Like the centipede," said Candace. "When it discovers it has a hundred legs, it stops being able to walk. That isn't true about centipedes, it turns out. Most don't have a hundred legs."

"Can I use that? When I'm over in Saratoga Springs?"

She looked at him sternly, an atmosphere of hers he particularly liked. Candace's mother had been so relentlessly ambitious, so determined to get out of her impoverished provincial Chinese village, that her school friends mocked her as "the toad who dreams of eating swan meat."

"You are taking this seriously? Send *me*, if you're not going to be serious about it. Vanessa's life—it isn't some silly English play."

Alan thought for a very brief moment about how poorly Candace's arrival in Saratoga Springs would be received.

"Of course I'm serious. But I can only be myself."

3

That self was in need of a bath, and later a drink or two. He turned on the taps in the main bathroom, the grand one he liked best—the one that would have to become his mother's if she moved in with them. He had a routine for bath-taking: as soon as he climbed into the tub, itself a decreasingly facile project, he emptied the water, so that he never spent more than four minutes immersed, and most of that time in mild discomfort. Da had instructed him in that particular hardship; it was the way a lad kept himself "hard." (Though Da's baths were also cold.) In the north of England, "hardness" mattered more than cleverness or beauty or gentleness. The young men like him would roll their shirtsleeves high, so their biceps showed like a ball emerging from a cannon. They nailed metal crescents—"segs"—into their shoe heels, so they could stomp and click and scrape hard military sparks from the pavement. He still conformed to his father's mindless code, and the rare bathing exception seemed like a great luxury: today he would sit for twenty good minutes in a warm bath whose waterline didn't immediately start wavering down to nothing.

He looked down as he stood by the bath: odd that his dick looked darker than the rest of his body, as if somehow it were older than the rest of him. *White meat or dark meat?* His chest hair, which when he was young had been like the tangled stuff on the

floor of a forest, was now blandly gray, and crisp like dried tobacco. Behold, the wanning. And what was so strange, or maybe
not that strange because he had friends who said the same,
was that when he looked at the mirror, a sixty-eight-year-old
Alan Querry did not look back, but little Alan, ten-year-old Alan,
twenty-year-old Alan. It was as if everything that had happened
to him between ten and sixty-eight had happened in a very small
set of rooms; as if childhood were just down the corridor, and
adolescence in that curious little cupboard off the kitchen, all of
it near at hand, not decades away, not houses or streets away, but
absolutely *near at hand*. Sixty-eight years—marriage, births, divorce, deaths, money—had taken no longer to live than the time
it took to cross from one side of that corridor to the other. Nothing
really had diminished, withered or waned or wanned, not sex,
nor the potential for happiness, nor curiosity. For three months
now, his life had been full of financial worry. The business was
shaky—they had clearly overextended themselves with the foolish
Dobson project—but on good days he still had the optimistic feeling that he could climb out of all this as one could just get out of
the bath, leaving the swill behind.

His dad had been optimistic like that—imperturbable, ro-
bustly good-natured, intelligent. He never saw his father shed a
tear, never once saw him lose his temper. His mother had had
some kind of nervous breakdown just after Alan was born; they
treated her in Newcastle with electric shock therapy. Maybe that
was where Van got her problems from? But Mam, at least, was
the source, the keeper of emotion in the family. She had the keys:
if she had died before Da, the gates to feeling would have been
shut. Alan and his father never spoke about feelings. It was Mam
who raged and cried and laughed. Emotion was female. But so
were joy and tenderness. Social aspiration, too—Mam's fake
"middle class" accent.

And now—he was sitting in the bath, steaming and spread-

ing like a sponge—he had to go in three days to Saratoga Springs,
to *be there* for his daughter, for poor Vanessa.

The first warning sign had come just before Christmas, when
Vanessa canceled a long-standing plan to come over to England
for the holiday. She wasn't feeling well, she had too much "work"
to do. Alan knew from long experience that Van's physical ail-
ments were rarely confined to the body, and that claims of "work"
covered many evasions and much nonproductivity. Then a few
weeks later, in early January, came the terrible e-mail from
Josh—sent only to Helen, but forwarded by her to Alan. Josh
said that Vanessa had slid into a deep depression in early Decem-
ber. Vanessa began to "withdraw" from him, "and withdraw
from *life*—that's how I would really put it." There had been what
he called "an incident," just before Christmas, when Vanessa fell
down some stairs and hurt her arm. Josh got scared: "I think she
was in danger of doing harm to herself." He said that she'd been
better in recent weeks, but was still pretty fragile, and he was
writing because he knew that Helen came to New York often for
business. When Helen was next in the city, would she think of
coming upstate, to Saratoga Springs? "You and your dad, of
course, know her 'history' so much better than I do."

Helen replied that she was in fact going to be in New York
City, for the record company, in early February; she could make
a trip upstate then, and she would try to bring Alan. And Alan,
perhaps because Josh had not written to him but to Helen, perhaps
because he was too afraid, too polite, too bloody English, had not
e-mailed to ask exactly what Josh meant when he suggested that
Vanessa's accident had been deliberate. "In danger of doing harm
to herself." Not this again: Alan had thought it belonged to the
past, had been left behind in Oxford, when Van was a student. If
she had tried to harm herself, it was clearly not for *real*, it was
just a "signal," a message, an SOS—isn't that what people said
about such gestures? While he also thought, with horror: but she

couldn't just toss her life aside, like an unfinished crossword puzzle . . . A father—a parent—helped his grown-up children in any way he could. He had known unhappiness, and some of it had been quite severe; but he didn't think he'd ever really known despair. Despair was of the spirit, it was terminal. Despair was the color blindness that afflicted those who could not see hope. Why did Helen find happiness easy, when her sister found it hard? The girls had always been so different. Perhaps Van's "history" went all the way back to birth. And then what could Alan possibly do? That had always been his torment; how little he could do. He couldn't make Van see life through his eyes: where he saw a white bird, she saw a black one. But of course he would come, of *course*. He would buy a plane ticket immediately, and he would go with Helen. It would be Van's belated Christmas gathering.

4

Vanessa and Helen, Helen and Vanessa . . . Vanessa was the elder by two years, born just after ten o'clock on the evening of July 30, 1966, the day England beat West Germany in the World Cup. The one and only time! You couldn't forget that day: those jubilant hours, the black-and-white television bringing forth its frail, unlikely pictures, and Cathy walking stiffly around the sitting room, pressing her hand into her lower back, her groans mixed now in his memory with the roars from Wembley Stadium—and there, a little later, Vanessa *was*, jaundiced and moist, furrowed with folds, most loved because the first. "Only the best for her." A lucky girl. But as she got older, she became harder to embrace, awkward, softly distant. She didn't or wouldn't *fit*—like Alice in Wonderland, either too tall or too short. It was the divorce that changed everything. After Cathy walked out, Vanessa *withdrew*. The girls dealt differently with that catastrophe. Always fierce, Helen sided with her father and accused her mother, who had, after all, left Alan for Another Man, of being "obsessed with sex." (She was only thirteen, poor thing.) Vanessa was different. She took no sides, just went quiet; seemed to absorb all the consequences of the event, and disappeared from sight. She was always upstairs in that damn bedroom of hers, where she lay on her bed and read: massively, widely, seriously—novels, poetry, philosophy, feminism,

even ecology. He had never heard of most of her authors; sometimes he thought she chose the most obscure people she could,
just to spite him.

In happier times, Alan and Cathy had loved to observe the
differences between their daughters. How often, in the evening,
when other conversation faltered, the two parents talked about
"the girls," with the kind of fanatical wonderment—monotonous
but somehow never boring!—that revolutionaries must lavish on
their plans for the future. Helen was exuberant, playful, dis-
obedient, physical; Vanessa was shy, gentle, slow to anger, studious,
very private. For a while, these differences seemed provisional, part
of the scramble' of growing up; everything was potential. But
eventually, so Alan discovered, the child's feet stop growing, her
trousers don't need to be let out anymore, her handwriting has the
form it will have for the rest of her life, her bedsheets bear the
occasional but unmistakable bloodstains of new adolescence—
and, as if suddenly, while you were not properly attending to the
matter (or so it seemed to him now), while you were too busy
with your own foolish crises, your daughter became an adult,
and those qualities that had seemed malleable were now hard-
ened and fixed. Both girls were full of will, but while Helen's
willfulness seemed to bring her pleasure, Vanessa's brought her
unhappiness. She seemed so keen to *mess up her own chances*.
That was the phrase he kept on reciting to himself in those days.
Why did she want to *mess up her own chances*? Why didn't Van
invite any school friends over to the house? Didn't she have any
friends? She said she wanted to put herself forward for the school
debating society, but it never happened. It was the same with the
school orchestra, the school play. All her pastimes were solitary:
reading, playing the piano or the flute, listening to music, writing
poems. (Poems mostly full of despair and lament: one of them
was especially horrifying, it seemed to be about some unrequited
crush on a boy, and it ended with a line he would never forget,
about wanting to "jump from a high wall onto a hard pavement";

these poems greatly alarmed her parents when they discovered them in a notebook hidden under her mattress.) Later, a student at Oxford, Vanessa decided that she would give away all her possessions; a friend was so worried about her stability that she reported her to the university health services, who contacted Alan and Cathy. Helen spoke so easily to adults, confident in her ability to charm; Vanessa held back, in a gesture that seemed to combine—worst of all worlds—judgment and fear. Helen was naturally joyful; Van needed to be reminded of that category of human experience. And one day, you realize that your children's differences are not only temperamental and biological, but also moral and political, that each has a very distinct worldview. One day—he remembered it well—you witness your elder daughter, now seventeen, firmly lecturing her younger sister about the misery of life and the cruelty of all human beings, of all life, holding up a book her father had no idea she possessed, George Ryley Scott's *History of Torture*, waving it around, and saying: "Read this, read this, Helen, and you won't have any doubts about it!"

Is that how it had been? Her childhood a torture?

5

Helen and Vanessa, Vanessa and Helen . . . Vanessa did her doctorate at Princeton—"because I'm stifled in Oxford, and they'll pay for me to be at Princeton, and they actually want me there"—and had been seven years teaching philosophy at Skidmore College; there was now a faint suggestion, like a breeze carrying a smell of rot with it, of a career stagnating. Of unfulfilled promise. There had been a few papers: one of them, which Alan understood to be about how to combine French philosophy and English analytic philosophy in order to make a great new product—like combining French grapes and English soil to make that questionable wine they were now producing in Kent?—did fairly well, and bounced around the conference circuit. But now she was forty, and there had been no "big book," and no advancement. The same faculty profile and atrocious snapshot sat on the departmental website for all these years—*these academics*, thought Alan—Vanessa's beautiful dark hair pulled harshly tight at the back into a scholarly bun, her lovely intelligent face obscured by hideous clock-sized spectacles, and that fixed bibliography, with the eternally dangling promise of "Four Essays on Personhood (forthcoming)." Alan couldn't imagine her in Saratoga Springs, New York. She told him that Skidmore College was one of the best private institutions in America, and she told him something about the town, about its history as a vacation resort, a nineteenth-century spa with healing waters: the Baden-Baden, the Vichy of upstate New York. It was full of parks and grand hotels; people still gambled and raced horses there, and there were handsome, wide streets. Five years ago, he was reading *Diamonds Are Forever*—he had been rereading all the Ian Fleming books, on a whim—and was chuffed to see that James Bond and Felix Leiter visited the famous horse track at the very same Saratoga Springs.

But he didn't go to see her. She came to him, and he imagined that she came to Northumberland every summer because she was keen to escape America, or New York State. In summer, in Northumberland, the sheep made their pleated, laugh-like noises and rubbed their wool onto the drystone walls, and the straight old Roman roads glimmered in the broad gentle light, and there was really no better place to be on earth. Last summer, she had come for the whole of August—he liked that very much. He left her alone for a few days, went down to London, and when he came back there she was, *still there*—sometimes in her old bedroom, lying diagonally on the bed in her usual way, reading a book, sometimes in the sitting room, or outside on the lawn in a deck chair, smoking, always with a book and a pen in hand, wearing those curious baggy trousers. Unlike Helen, Vanessa seemed to need very little. She wanted to be at home, to be intermittently alone, and to be able to work. Little else. From the back door, he could see her in the deck chair, notebook open, pen in hand, cigarette packet and lighter on the grass beside her coffee cup; she'd got a bit heavier in the last year, perhaps the curious wafting trousers were hiding that. She slouched in the chair, her tongue slightly protruding. The notebook was balanced on her knees, and with her right hand she intensely twirled her hair, as if twisting thoughts from her brain. If Candy seemed to be asleep when meditating, Vanessa seemed almost to be posing as a thinker. She rarely wrote anything: fascinating, the ratio of thought to frequency of writing. She was like a trumpeter playing Haydn in a symphony, picking up the instrument only every hundred bars or so. Aphorisms, maybe? Philosophical fragments? It would be funny if she were just writing jokes, or writing a letter, or doodling aimlessly. And though he knew he shouldn't, he would go out and disturb her, offer her some more coffee, ask her if she needed anything from Corbridge, tell her one of his own jokes, to match those in her notebook.

Had she really tried to do herself some harm in Saratoga Springs? Put aside her life—he kept coming back to this image—like a half-finished crossword puzzle? Of course, thought Alan, Josh had been deliberately vague with Helen, when he described the incident on the stairs, probably because he wanted to ration the alarm—enough to get them to come, but not so much that they would insist on taking Vanessa home with them. Josh must love her, then; he was possessive in the right way, watchful in the right way—and obviously kind. Alan thought the e-mail reflected pretty well on the young man.

After Vanessa ran away from boarding school, Alan and Cathy decided that she should "see someone" about her depression and anxiety. They found a child therapist in Newcastle, who was attached in some way to the teaching hospital there. She was hard to find, he remembered. *No one* had "therapy" in Newcastle in 1982! And Vanessa did not want to go, had to be almost dragged into the grim office on Percy Street. Worse, much worse, the therapist—her last name was Lennon, like John—insisted that she see the whole family for the first session. All of them, even Helen. Alan and Cathy had been separated for eight months and had stopped communicating, except to talk about matters relating to the girls. Alan sat there in a fury as Dr. Lennon told them that she was going to use a tape recorder; she found it useful to listen to them talking—to detect, after the session, their recorded hesitations and evasions and weaknesses and lies. Of course, she didn't put it quite like that, but that was the gist: *cherchez* the parents, find out how the parents were to blame, and stitch them

up. And they *were* to blame. Of course they were. Poor, poor
Vanessa—she cried and cried, while the little gap-toothed wheels
of the Memorex cassette squeakily rotated, while Alan and Cathy
tried to explain how hard things had been for both girls. (And
yet Helen did not cry, did she?) Dr. Lennon then had four ses-
sions with Van on her own, and when it was all over, she called in
the despicable parents, and explained that she couldn't of course
share any details of what Vanessa had told her—just what *had*
Van told her?—but she could certainly inform them that in her
opinion their elder daughter was extremely anxious, and "severely
depressed." The therapist recommended that Vanessa write about
her fears and sadness, in creative form. Alan didn't mention that
Van was already doing that . . .

Van did get better; happier, more fulfilled in her academic
work, drawn—drawn *out*—by the task of serious philosophy.
The last two years of school, and the first year at Oxford, were
comparatively serene. (Everything was comparative, in Van's
case.) But then she collapsed again—in her final year at Oxford—
and tried to give away all her possessions to her friends, and had
to be brought home by Helen, and at that time she spoke of being pursued by what she called her "demons." Had she intended
to harm herself at Oxford? Was she thinking of . . . suicide? He
could hardly bear to think, let alone speak, that word. He had to
look away from it, as from the sun. And perhaps it was true, he
now thought, that because he looked away from *that* word, he
had also looked away from the other word, *depression*. He looked
away, and by the time Van was in her mid-twenties, Alan had
decided that most of Vanessa's problems were not really chronic,
but largely related to her solitude. She never seemed to have a boyfriend, she read books all day (hard, systematically unhelpful
books, as he saw it). She took no exercise, never went for a walk
or a bike ride. Ma wasn't correct when she said that if Josh was
"the one," Alan would blame the lad for taking his daughter
away. Not at all: he welcomed Josh with relief. The news about a

boyfriend was received as another parent might receive news
about a child's new job or first house. And the truth was, Vanessa
had been much happier in recent months, since she and Josh
started going out in June; she was full of new projects and resolve,
as he saw in the summer when she sat happily in the deck chair,
carefully answering her philosophical riddles. He tried hard to
keep this summery Vanessa in his mind, not the girl who disappeared for two days when she was fifteen; or who refused to get
out of bed for what seemed like a whole month when she was
twenty-one; or who very nearly abandoned her Ph.D. four years
later and spoke seriously about opening an organic restaurant in
Corbridge; or who was about to turn down the offer of the
assistant professorship at Skidmore and come home to England
without a job, "because what's the point of teaching philosophy?"

What he strongly remembered today was walking with
Vanessa when she was five or six, past the medieval church in the
village, the church which flew a red-on-white St. George's flag
from its tower. In the northern wind, the flapping cloth pulled
away from the metal pole like a young soldier eager to dash into
battle. That day, it was at half-mast, and little Vanessa, happy
Vanessa, asked him what that meant. Someone prominent had
died, he said. For several years afterward, when they went past
the church and the flag was back at full-mast, Van would look
up and announce with satisfaction: "No one died today."

6

Helen had it worked out. Tart, humorous, and always very efficient, she e-mailed him a bristling itinerary. She was already in Manhattan, where she'd been for a few days, on the record company's shilling. (He imagined a prairie-sized hotel suite, loaded with goodies.) He would fly on British Airways, London to New York, spend the night at a hotel he'd never heard of on Park Avenue, the same one that Helen was staying in, and the next morning they would take the 8:15 train from Penn Station to Saratoga Springs. Helen could only spend three days with him—she had little Jack and little Oliver, and big Tom, to get back to in London, and big Tom, though thirty-seven years old, was presently as babyish and self-absorbed as the three-year-old twins. Alan was staying for six days. She reminded him to take his laptop, the melatonin she'd given him a few months earlier, his sleeping pills, and a pair of sunglasses ("counterintuitive and counterseasonal, but you'll understand when you see American sunlight on snow"). He packed the thing he was currently reading about the Big Bang, and two new books from Candace, one about Zen Buddhism by the man with the same first name as him, and a popular Chinese psychiatric guide to decoding your dreams. The problem with the Chinese dream book was that most of the analyzed dreams featured dragons, doves, and pigs, rather than, say, strangely faceless but arousing women, or Cathy. (Though page 23, and this could be useful, told him that a dream featuring doors meant that his children would be "unsuccessful.")

He flew from Newcastle to Heathrow, and had lunch at the caviar bar in Terminal 4, an allowable luxury. The airport was like a fancy hospital, patients ambling up and down the bright corridors, pushing their medical apparatuses, fatalistic and expectant at once. They popped into Gucci and Prada for preflight necessities. His smoked salmon was very good. They knew how to do things in London, even if they squirted the dill mustard onto the plate from a large plastic bottle. He was thirty-six before he ever tasted smoked salmon, so had no guilt at all, he was making up for lost time. Next to him, rather astonishingly, a man seemed to be sacking a junior employee—gently, sympathetically, warmed by Sancerre, and with pauses to allow him to transfer fresh sheets of pinkish salty tissue from the plate to his fat mouth. Alan leaned closer, as he generally did in such situations. Nowadays, people seemed to enjoy being eavesdropped on, even spoke a bit louder when they knew there was a chance of being overheard.

Alan was in fact quite excited to see his daughters in a new country, so he had to remind himself from time to time that no one was exactly on holiday. Death had made him a Little Englander: he'd only left the country a handful of times since Cathy died twelve years ago. He blamed himself for being out of the country when she finally succumbed to the cancer that had taken so long to plot its steady theft. He'd been in Lisbon, enjoying the warmth, the suffused light, when Helen phoned with the news . . . Anyway, America was hardly the country he would have chosen for a family vacation. America had never attracted him much. He had watched, with bemusement, his daughters go off there to work or to travel. It sometimes seemed as if in the last thirty years of his life, the little island nation that he grew up in, which for centuries had generated its own history and literature and record of prodigious scientific and industrial innovation, not to mention a fairly eventful politics, had meekly let the Americans come and restock the shelves with their own merchandise. No one objected that American presidential elections, American music, American money, American movies, American technology, and God help us, American food constituted the new reality. (Yes, it was as if the British Isles had turned in the sea, like a child's boat in a bath, had turned slightly but definitively, away from Europe toward America.) He had quite happy memories of his only trip to the States, twenty-one years ago, on business. Three days in crazy New York, and then a day "relaxing" in some fancy dull suburb outside the city, where the only sounds between nine and six were the workers' Spanish, and chestnuts falling gently onto the ridiculously wide, empty streets. People always seemed to be hoping he would "have a good day" (*Actually, I have other plans*). He did sincerely love—and rate as one of the great American contributions—the phrase "Take it easy." He'd heard that from a taxi driver, from a guy in a shop, even from an air stewardess. Take it easy! That benign blessing wouldn't catch on in Britain, where the pavements were sopped with cold rainwater and everyone seemed to have attended queuing school, to learn how to do it with the requisite degree of resigned submission.

But he had to admit that America had never quite *existed* for him. He'd read somewhere that Americans used, per capita, three times as many sheets of toilet paper a day as the global average, which told him what he needed to know. It was an enormous, religious, largely reactionary place, with no real tradition of socialism, where the car parks were larger than many European villages. And Americanism was so bloody contagious! First George Bush's born-again Christianity and his terrible Iraq crusade, and then Tony Blair's American-style religiosity. Apparently, no one in the States had ever encountered Samuel Johnson's dictum—banged into him by Mr. Watson ("Clag"), his school history teacher—that patriotism is the last refuge of a scoundrel.

7

Snowfall had covered the city two days earlier. The cold was exotic—shockingly comprehensive, absolute. At JFK, he shuddered his way to the taxi rank. Was it possible that Helen might come from the city to meet him at the terminal? Okay, it was ... not, but he indulged the fantasy for a few minutes as he emerged from customs.

The cold made everything rigid. He was amazed by the icy fossilized hardness, the cars and buses caked in white salt, as if dug out of a quarry, the roads littered with ice, salt, rubbish, everything streaked and blanched. Exhaust fumes hung whitely, painted onto the polar air. But people were shouting as if they were in the hottest tropics. The tall black bloke who looked like a policeman, with a sort of padded orange eiderdown that went all the way to his shoes, was shouting at the taxi drivers, who shouted back at him, and the customers were shouting at each other as crafty ones tried to jump the queue. Now the black bloke was pointing at him and yelling "Fourth car, fourth car!" and he stumbled quickly to a large yellow Ford, and they were off, and it wasn't very different from how he remembered it twenty years before. The surging of the cab, as if prodding itself into battle, the wasteful slippage of the big automatic V8, the sadistic achievement of the raked partition, which made every back-seat traveler a giant in a plastic bathtub, the embattled roads and laughable neglected bridges, on which moved the latest German cars, suddenly futuristic and anomalous. Those fine new European cars, metal cockroaches, will survive the American apocalypse.

The sense of having dropped into the middle of a civil war, with Manhattan as the wrecked spoils.

It was a long way from the quiet stone house in Northumberland, though not unexciting. A long sour tunnel, and suddenly with a few large bumps they were in the middle of the city, which was like heaven and hell combined, infernal but glittering with lights. The forced march of the skyscrapers, herded into groups. But the regime of verticality gave way, on Park Avenue south of Grand Central Station, to a more easygoing administration: he felt he could breathe among the shorter buildings, the apartment buildings, the galleries, even a church or two. His hotel was in fact opposite a church, Orthodox perhaps. As he got out of the cab and looked up Park Avenue, the massive old Pan Am tower, now renamed something else, seemed like a dam that was keeping the crazy tide of Midtown from flowing south.

The hotel lobby was small, gold, and comfortable. Expensive. Helen looked after herself—well, the record company looked after its executives. He got to his room, though not easily, because the corridor was sunk in a deliberate and possibly *perfumed* designer gloom, and sat on the bed. Asked to be put through to Helen Querry. Certainly sir, room 432—engaged. Of course. Ten minutes: time for a shit, and a Scotch from the minibar. In that order. Room 432, please. Still engaged. So he would part the darkness and make his own way to her. She knew when he was coming in. On the fourth floor he groped along the row of glow-worm room numbers. And knocked on the door—why on earth was he a tiny bit nervous?

Helen opened the door, blew him a kiss, pointed at the un-cradled phone and returned to it, standing with it in one hand while she examined the BlackBerry she held in the other. She rolled her eyes at him in self-absolution: the sin of work. There she was, and my, she did look good. "Well for God's sake, get him to weaponize those fabled 'media contacts' of his! It's being released next month, we need all the help we can get. Yes, he's got plenty . . . Yep. Okeydokey. Ciao." He disliked both "okey-dokey" and "ciao."

"Dad, you *got* here . . ."

"I came by the same means as you, you know." The last words came out a little closer to "you knaw" than he would have liked. Helen's accent was placeless but not classless: upper-middle class, not quite upper class, southern, boarding-school. (What he wanted to call *wine bar posh*, if that made sense.) Undeniably the best thing he'd given his daughters was the entitlement never to think about social class. Now she was looking at him, appraising him—warmly but with a sharp eye, as if he were back in the nursing home with his ma. But she was, brilliantly, doing this while also reading something on her BlackBerry.

"Is that shirt new?"

"Are you talking to me or to that screen?" He was smiling.

"I'm sorry."

"It's newish. Why, don't you like it?"

"I do like it."

He wasn't sure that he liked it that much, in fact. He felt the need to assert himself, take the upper hand—but why was he thinking like this?

"Right, are we going to have dinner somewhere, or what?"

"I've booked a place two blocks away. Just let me close down these things." Swiftly, elegantly, she tattooed the little device in her hand with a single finger, slipped it into her beautiful mustard-colored handbag, then crossed the room—now he noticed properly that it was much bigger than his—to the desk that held her laptop. She knelt before it, and it looked as if she was about to make herself up at a mirror. A little more tapping; not so easy to dislodge herself from this screen.

They went down into the marble and brass lobby, and the doorman eased them out into the astonishing cold. New York met them like another dimension. There was something almost comical about the exchange of opposites: noise and cold for silence and warmth. A fire engine was bucking down Park Avenue, clanking its chains like an angry ghost, and it was impossible to speak or think while its siren warped the freezing air beside them. Helen took his arm, with that easy warmth she had. He relaxed a little, maybe for the first time since Josh's e-mail.

"How's work been?" he yelled at her. She shook her head, to signal "not well," perhaps, or more likely to hint that dialogue could wait until they reached the restaurant. She was so casually in charge. She came to New York five or six times a year. Vanessa lived in America, but in some ways Helen seemed more naturally at ease with Americans, did business with them, went to hear new bands, had twice been to Saratoga Springs in fact, to hear the Dave Matthews Band, a group that had made her, or Sony rather, a fair amount of money. She sped up and down the Sony skyscraper on Sixth Avenue. She nosed around the city in gurgling Lincoln Town Cars, spent weekends at a "legendary" record producer's house in Amagansett, where there were two pools, a six-car garage, and a basement kitted out with the largest collection of 1960s jukeboxes on the Eastern Seaboard. He'd heard some of her stories; he'd once actually met Dave Matthews, a polite, well-educated bloke whose residual Johannesburg accent was still just audible. He had great respect for her achievement. He could never do what she did, it was so social, involved so much arse-licking and party-going and drinking. And what else? Well, gambling, for one thing. Property was a sure and stable bet, stodgy compared to taking a punt on a rock band or solo singer. Buildings that failed to come up to business expectations were *still there*; you could use them for something, sell them at a loss, rent them until the market picked up, use them (however sneakily) as collateral, for more loans. They belonged to him, he *made* them, as surely as the men who put one brick on top of another and spread the muck, the mortar—the gobbo, the shite—between them. Helen, going up and down her great mortgaged tower in that glass elevator, didn't own the bands she undoubtedly helped to make. There must have been thirty "artists" whose first records came out, with a bit of juice from Sony or from one of its affiliate labels, and then . . . ran out of juice. Reasonable reviews, modest sales—and no contract renewal. One of them, Verity McQueen, whose music he listened to when he drove along the A68 to see his mum, was now teaching singing at a private girls' school in London. The girls she taught knew nothing about her brilliant first album, knew nothing about her aborted career as a singer-songwriter, said Helen; it was too long ago, and for kids nowadays the past, as Vanessa lamented about her students at Skidmore, was nothing more than the tree that fell in the forest when you weren't there.

8

The restaurant was bullish and manic. And the young waiter was offhand and woundingly ugly. It wasn't his fault, obviously, but somehow his ugliness seemed a weapon of his rudeness. His elaborate facial hair—facial topiary, really—made Helen think of the dreaded face-painting that went on at her kids' parties: scrawled lions' manes and tiger whiskers, difficult to remove whatever the kindhearted and absurdly patient teenage volunteers claimed. She was irritated that the place was so loud (Toto, of all things, on the sound system), the service so casual and juvenile. Roger, her impeccably tailored young assistant in London, had done some research: it was new, it was very near the hotel, had had good reviews for its French-Cambodian-American, whatever that was, food. But they'd have been better off eating in the dim, cave-like hotel restaurant. This was exactly the sort of place Dad hated—basically a noisy gym with food, everybody toned, young, and fuck-off fit.

Alan's gray head shone singly, as if spotlit. He looked knackered, she thought, but maybe that was just airports and jet lag. His jacket sleeves—a tiny bit too long. I must see him more often than I do. But not if that involves going up to Northumberland. To Candyland.

Yet he was smiling at her, as if to say, I know what you're

thinking, there's no need to apologize for the restaurant, these things happen, we're in New York, after all . . .

"We're in New York!"

"Yes, Dad, a bit painfully—I'm sorry. You won't be able to hear anything I say."

"You may have buggered up your hearing with all those concerts, but *my* hearing is fine." His lips silently shaped: "I'M SHOUTING AT YOU BUT YOU CAN'T HEAR ME!"

"Ha-ha, very funny, Dad."

He continued: "NO, REALLY, I'M SHOUTING AT YOU." It was a family tradition that Alan's jokes went on too long— like, she now thought, an alarm you fumbled to switch off in the morning.

"No, but seriously" (the snooze button had been located), "I like the noise, I don't mind missing a bit here and there. Selective deafness might be useful up in Saratoga?"

"Springs. Saratoga Springs. Saratoga is somewhere else. Florida, I think."

"Yep, I know that name."

"But let's talk about that later, no?"

"Okay."

The waiter arrived, with two bowls of olive oil and several torn pillows of artisanal loaf.

"What have you been doing in New York?"

"Oh God, too much, it's been absolutely *crazy* here, it's always like this. Lots of big meetings, a lot of corporate and legal bullshit—the Americans are very good at looking after you, they do things properly, but you have to work for it, work, work. They do love their eight a.m. breakfast meetings! I'm . . . I'm quite a big deal here, actually . . ."

"I'm not at all surprised."

"They make a fuss of me."

"What's that?"

"They make a *fuss* of me, they look after me very well."

"Yes, so they should, so they should . . . Do you actually *like* New York?"

"Well, I don't want to live here, if that's what you mean."

He didn't really know what he meant; he just felt slightly argumentative.

"All this flashy money and noise," he added.

"You just said you liked it!"

"I do, but I always feel that something is going to fall on my head."

"Icicles do sometimes come down in this season. A student was killed a few years ago. Look, I enjoy the city, though much less since the kids were born, I certainly can't imagine trying to bring up children here . . . They're fine, by the way, Dad! . . . And Tom sends his love . . . I like it, and I like how straightforward Americans are, in the business world. There's none of that tiresome English hand-wringing, that subterfuge, the perpetual apologies. *More money, less crap*: that's the simple reason why Europeans come over and work here. Isn't it? Also, Sony have been great employers."

"Have been . . . ?"

Speaking to her father about work, she always made sure to emphasize the business side: a storm of meetings and deals, indistinguishable from banking or the law. The hours spent flat on her back, headphones on, listening to rubbishy hopeful recordings, all the anxiety when a new record was being released, the immense amount of organizing and electronic paperwork—*that* we ignore, because Dad, apart from a few quiet songs by Pink Floyd and one particular eccentric thing by Ian Dury, had never had time for contemporary music, for *her* music. Dad thought her colleagues all looked and acted like Leon Russell at the Concert for Bangladesh, i.e., circa 1971—the crazy white beard and the long hair. "These blokes," he once said, looking over her shoulder at a copy of *Melody Maker* with a photo of someone *like* Eric Clapton but not Eric Clapton, in mid-solo, head thrown back, "look, it's just male exhibitionism, mating rituals—he's holding his penis out in one hand"—he pointed at the neck of the guitar—"and strumming his balls with the other." Maybe not the most original observation, but you didn't forget it when *your dad* was the one saying it. This was the time when Dad was noticing such things. Having failed to groom Vanessa—bespectacled, unkempt, even a bit smelly in those days—Dad turned his attention to Helen, told her what "looked good" on her, told her that "you know you're attractive when male drivers stop in busy traffic to let you cross the road" (a truth annoyingly hard to dismiss), praised himself for never spending more than four minutes in the bath, of all the silly male vanities . . . The strange thing was that though he could be, on occasion, a male bore and a selfish shit, he was not innately those. At that time, he seemed to be playing the *role* of patriarch, as if someone were paying him to act it out. But later she understood why: it was not so long after Mum moved out and went to live with the repellent Patrick Needham, and Dad was still angry and terribly insecure, his wounds flowing . . .

The waiter arrived to take orders, and complimented them on their excellent taste: "*Very* good choices." He pronounced "Madam" as "Madame."

"Well, I'll be the judge of that," said Alan once they were alone.

"Of what?"

"Of whether I've made a good choice."

"It's a weird American mania—it's catching on in London. You now get praised for everything. For having a birthday or ordering a meal or having finished your year at school, or just buying something really expensive in a shop."

They started eating.

"I can't help thinking, though," Helen continued, "does he do that with everyone, even when there are six people at a table? I mean, we can't all be making identically good choices, can we?"

"Sounds like a philosopher's job."

They looked at each other. This wasn't the place to talk about Vanessa, she thought as the music—something she knew but couldn't now name—loudly worked the room.

It would have to wait, Alan thought—the *conversation*. Christ, he was tired.

9

———

He'd said goodnight to Helen, and now wasn't sleepy, half-naked on his hotel bed. A powerful impulse arose whenever Alan spent time with one of his daughters— he immediately wanted to speak to the other about the one he'd just seen. Helen and Vanessa, Vanessa and Helen . . . And what would he say now to Van? That Helen seems tired, overworked, but not especially keen to return to Tom; that for some reason— despite what must be a very good income—she's worried about money but hiding it well; that something weird is going on at Sony (thanks to Helen, it "somehow" hadn't come up again at dinner); that she was cross at herself for choosing the wrong restaurant and wouldn't really admit the mistake (how he enjoyed "forgiving" her for that). He wouldn't tell Vanessa that men—certain men, or more precisely men of a certain age—looked twice, looked three times at Helen, and that he didn't so much mind being mistaken for her seedy older husband or boyfriend.

He glanced at his wide feet: the littlest toe of each foot was not quite right, a birth defect, slightly squashed or deformed, as if crushed by one of the other little piggies on its way to market . . . It was 4:00 a.m. in Northumberland, too early even for sleepless Candace. He pointed the remote at the gigantic looming TV, hanging like a vertical table, the place at which everyone now meets for hospitality, and jabbed at the buttons with not very expert fingers. The colors were more garish than on English telly—a violent brightness in the lighting (a leathery man and a pretty woman at a news desk, virulent reds and blues behind them, the news crawl along the bottom of the screen just obscuring the woman's breasts). He flicked through five, seven, eight channels. American television seemed to be an endless procession of local news programs in which people kept on promising weather forecasts. They were clearly far more obsessed about the weather than the British. He tried a few times to get an actual forecast, and then gave up, muted the volume and lay on the bed—Scotch in one hand and his book on Zen Buddhism in the other.

10

It had been impossible to sleep—hot air exploded into the room at unreliable intervals, and trucks seemed to be collecting rubbish all night outside his window—but oddly he felt quite rested when he met Helen for breakfast. There she sat, as she used to at home, eating nothing of course, drinking sweet black coffee, very straight in her chair, exact and controlled—and how he loved her: her slightly thick shoulders (Cathy), her longish nose (his), the light amusement around her mouth (the sardonic grimace his mum was so good at), and Cathy's thin lips. He loved even her impatience, it was so familiar. He would have to say, as he now did, "I think we've got plenty of time, there's no hurry," and she would have to say, as she now did, "I never said a thing about being in a hurry."

Every time he saw his daughters, he experienced such hunger for them, and the hunger was so simply satisfied that he was freshly amazed that he didn't see them more. That extraordinary power family had, to blot out all other considerations, all other desires and dissatisfactions: perhaps he'd feared that, recognized its engrossing fanaticism. If you surrendered to that, you would do nothing else in life, build nothing else. And there had always been the company alongside the family—the *company*, that word the poor kids heard probably every day when they were young. A word they must have learned to tiptoe around, as if past the closed door of a sickroom. *I'm doing it for the company! If the company goes down, then everything goes down with it! Look, I've built a bloody company, it takes effort!*

"Don't tell me: you slept atrociously. It was too hot, you couldn't open the window, and the garbage trucks came along at four in the morning, which sounded like bombs going off just outside your window." Helen had the blue amusement again in her eyes.

"Actually, not bad at all. I feel pretty good."

"Well, I slept fairly badly. And according to Tom this morning the twins both have terrible colds."

"Oh no—I'm so sorry to hear that . . . But you wouldn't go back now?" He said it a little too needily; he couldn't make the trip to Vanessa on his own.

"Absolutely not. Let Tom deal with it for once. Don't worry: I'm here for the weekend, as promised."

●

They walked from the hotel—less shockingly cold today, though he still needed his woolen cap. They both pulled little wheelie cases, and the doubled noise of the coarse plastic granulation on the pavement caused New Yorkers to look round, though never actually to make any space for them. Their words expired in steam.

He was walking a little faster than he wanted to. Alongside Helen, he always had the sense of a tall woman taking long strides. At the mouth of the station—hideously chaotic, with once again a lot of pointless American yelling—she took his arm and gently steered him onto the escalator, and they went down into what appeared to be a depressed underground shopping mall: a dirty-looking pharmacy (a contradictory combination in Europe), a Krispy Kreme doughnut franchise, a shuttered Staples, the air heavy with smells of cinnamon, cheese, and . . . vomit? A local train must have arrived, and suddenly he and Helen were pushing against thick waves of commuters, thousands of rank-and-filers, most of them marching—to judge from the earbuds and head-phones—to the beat of their own drums. The floor seemed to shake, and he was glad to join a docile queue for the "Adiron-dack" train to Albany and Saratoga Springs.

"Is it possible you've never been, Dad, on an American train?"

"It is possible."

"Well, fasten your seat belt."

And then they were descending again, by narrow escalator, and at the platform they climbed up into a carriage that looked like some futuristic design from one of the boys' comics he used to love: ribbed silver steel, a horizontal rocket, the windows de-fensively small, the wheels massive. The locomotive was a solid primitive block of engine. To open the heavy carriage doors, you kicked a spring-loaded magic trigger. Inside the carriage, there was a large vacated space of plastic and cloth in autumnal browns and oranges. The seats were twice as wide as in an English train. Hot air roared from rattling circular vents that resembled plastic drains. The train started, then stopped again. Started once more, accelerated coarsely, as they swayed through sooty tunnels. They were moving at about the pace of an old English steam train on a rural route. In 1951, when he and his parents had made the great trip to London, his first—for the Festival of Britain exhibition—the steam train reached ninety miles an hour . . . He was twelve. A little boy in gray short trousers . . . dressed in his school uniform, because everything else was too worn and there wasn't enough money to buy him a new jacket. He wasn't self-conscious, was proud actually, it looked as if he was going to London to receive some kind of prize or scholarship, and the uni-form was distinguished (a St. Cuthbert's cross in silver wire on the breast pocket). He felt like a little lord in it. Acted like one, too. His parents often told the story of how Uncle Dan (the only person in his family to make any money, before he did) once took him for a fancy afternoon tea at the Royal County Hotel in

Durham. The posh hotel. Little Alan was dressed in his school
uniform; with a princely gesture, he handed his school cap to the
bellboy at the door; and the bellboy, probably only ten years older
than he was, meekly accepted that cap and looked after it until
tea was over . . . In London, no one looked twice at the little boy
in his uniform. But it didn't matter, once he got to the Festival of
Britain site. It was on the South Bank, next to the river. The
Thames was right there, sluggish and brown with history, and
the huge exhibition looked over it, in rebuke: because the Festival was the Future! All the boys his age made straight for the
Science Dome, where 1950s-style robots snapped up and down
the length of an enormous hall, and you could put your head right
into the jet engine (invented by the Englishman Frank Whittle)
of a de Havilland Vampire, the RAF jet fighter that arrived just
too late to do anything useful in the war. There were stalls about
amphibious vehicles, electric cars, new helicopters, and a plane
that could take off and land vertically like a helicopter. Thrillingly,
an engineer in a white coat selected Alan and another boy for the
Great Radar Game. In a dark room, the boys got to look at a
screen full of moving dots, a mock-up of a typical night during
the Blitz, the dots representing German bombers. With a click
of a switch, the two boys destroyed every single plane as if they
were clay pigeons, and saved London. And after those excite-
ments (with a boring wander around the exhibit on the history of
English gardens, endured for the sake of his mother—but now
gardening was *his* great adult passion . . .), there was a big afternoon tea at the Turntable Café, which rotated through 360 degrees
in the course of every hour, and was decorated with thousands of
gramophone records.

   He could see that old world so well, despite all the decades
that had passed: everyone in their browns, blacks, and grays.
People overlapped, resembled each other more closely than nowadays. The men, in those high-waisted baggy trousers, had a way

of putting their hands in their pockets and thrusting their hips forward—a little womanishly, he now thought. Everyone was more modest—in expression, in expectation. Food was still being rationed: he remembered the moment, two or three years later, when Uncle Dan brought something out of a packet and said to him, "Do you know what these are?" Alan looked blankly at the handful of small, chipped, irregular sand-colored pebbles, and shook his head. Uncle Dan exclaimed with complacent triumph: "They're peanuts." On the way back from the London exhibition, he was very hungry but there was nothing to eat. He remembered that, being hungry. Still, the steam train went amazingly fast, storming and burning its tremendous way through the soft countryside.

"Does it go any quicker than this?" They had left New York, and the Hudson River was gleaming through trees.

"Not much . . . but you hardly ever get the big accidents that happen in Europe. I actually get fearful when these trains try to go fast! You can get lots of work done, because the journeys are always so long."

"Well, don't let me stop you." She already had her laptop out anyway. He couldn't compete with an electronic screen.

"Do you need to get stuff done, too?" she asked.

"Nothing that can't wait. I'd like at some point to talk about Vanessa." It sounded more formal than he wanted it to.

"Of course," she said in a businesslike way, as if it were a necessary, rather poorly paid chore. "Let's do that now, so that we have a bit of a plan for the days ahead."

"I hope we don't need a *plan*, exactly," he said, thinking that indeed they did need some sort of plan. "It's not that bad, is it?"

"I have no idea. But for instance, neither of us knows Josh, though we've been through versions of this a few times now with Vanessa, over the years." She glanced blandly at the laptop screen.

"She just needs us, at the moment, which is why we're here."

"Oh, Dad, I wish it were that simple!"

"I didn't say it is simple. Christ, *you're* not simple either."

"But you remember the first 'episode'? When she ran away from school? It was Vanessa responding belatedly to the divorce. We can see that now. And yes, it was a very difficult time for everyone, but why did she deal with it so differently from you and me? We just got on with it. She went to a billion pieces—and the way she attacked *me* at the time, as if *I* was the cause of it all."

"But maybe the logical thing, after all that sadness, *was* to go to pieces?"

"Well then she needed to take it out on you or on Mum, not on me." She looked again at the screen; her fingers hovered over the keyboard, a pianist about to start a performance. Alan was hurt that she had said "on you or on Mum." It was Cathy who walked out, Cathy who had the affair, Cathy who left him with two young daughters.

Calmer, he wondered if Helen's anger was partly formulaic. To sound exasperated was how Helen felt she *should* sound. For so long now, the closed circuit of their relationship had been that Helen *did* things while Vanessa *thought* things. In fact, as Alan knew, Helen was tender, generous, even sentimental. During that first "episode," Vanessa ran away from her boarding school in Shropshire. Alan got a phone call, it was Vanessa's housemistress, the formidable Miss Plummer, a classicist whose first name, wonderfully, was Athena, and who had once firmly told Alan, when he inquired about the point of learning ancient Greek at a modern English girls' school: "The *point*? The point, of course, is to read Herodotus in the original!" Athena Plummer said that Vanessa had been missing for eight hours. If she didn't turn up by 7:00 p.m., the school would call the police. Miss Plummer had an idea that Vanessa might be making her way north, to her parents' house. Alan didn't have the heart to tell this unworldly woman that home was probably the last place on earth that Vanessa wanted to go. She had taken a bus to Bristol, in search of an older girl who had left the school a year earlier and was at university there; spent a couple of days sleeping on the student's floor, and then phoned home. It was Helen, extraordinarily mature for her thirteen years, who spoke to Vanessa, and persuaded her to go back to school; and when it emerged that the headmistress would decide Vanessa's fate, her status at the school imperiled not just because she had run away but because—this was a bit murky—she might have taken another girl's transistor radio with her, it was Helen who carried the family typewriter to her bedroom and wrote an intimate letter to the headmistress, laying out the family situation, her parents' separation, the finalization of the divorce, Vanessa's sadness and anger, and how Helen herself had felt several times like running away, too. Helen did not know that her father had seen the letter; the school's headmistress sent it to him, with a note calling it "remarkable." It was beautifully "remarkable." Alan had to control himself while reading it.

"That's all old history," he said quietly, "ancient times. What should we do when we get to Saratoga Springs? I mean, how . . . bad do you think she is?"

"How bad? I'm a bit sick of grading Vanessa's collapses, assessing the ferocity of 'the demons,' you know? Giving each drama its review. Maybe for once it would be nice not to be in the audience at all?"

He said nothing, just closed his eyes, and she took his hand and held his middle fingers.

"Why am I here, then? That's what you're thinking. I'm sorry . . . But, you know—Newtonian law, for every action there's a reaction . . . Look, I forwarded the e-mail to you. That's why we're both here."

"What did Josh mean when he talked about Van's 'history'? Do you think she's told him everything—going all the way back?"

"Dad, it's okay, you're not under surveillance! *You're* not the subject."

"What happened on the stairs? Was it an accident? I should have written to Josh."

"I don't exactly know, but it sounds, to me, like another of Vanessa's performances," said Helen.

"For goodness sake, Van has certainly 'surprised' us over the years, but I'd like to think that I don't have a daughter who throws herself down the stairs just because she damn well feels like it."

"Oh, Dad, I know you're angry."

"I'm not angry."

"All right, if you say so . . . I don't know whether it was just an accident. But I know that something has happened in the last few months that has been enough to frighten Vanessa's first boy-friend in many years. Will that do? That's why I'm here. What we can do is not be scared or angry, and find out what's behind all this. Or under it."

"I'm very glad you're here," he said. She was still holding his fingers, for him a wonderful childish forgetfulness. Then she detached, and turned.

"You know I almost left Tom two years ago? Almost just walked out with the twins?"

"No, of course I didn't know that. How could I, if you . . ."

"Well I'm telling you now, and . . . *just saying*. And now you know."

"Okay. What do you want to tell me about it? Anything?"

"No, because it never happened. I could have created an al-mighty fucking drama."

"Please don't," he said firmly, as if she were a little child about to fiddle with a fragile object. She looked at the rather prim alarm on his face and started to smile, and he couldn't help smil-ing a little uncertainly back at her.

"I won't, because we've *patched things up*. As they say. I actually don't want to break up my whole family." There was a long pause. "Anyway, it's not Tom I want to leave, it's Sony."

"Sony?"

"It's a long thing to tell. I don't want to bore you with it."

"No, yes—go on."

"Okay: I want to start my own company. Like you did. Remember that spat I had with Andy Farwell?"

"Andy . . . ?"

"Yes, Dad, Andy, do you listen to anything I tell you? Andy Farwell, my direct boss in London."

"Oh yes, okay." As far as he was concerned, her colleagues blended into a single suspect mass.

"Well, I came *that* close to quitting, you remember? I come into work on a Monday morning, and I find that the extremely long memo I had spent *weeks* on, about the future of the music industry, really important stuff actually, but what *they* were soporifically calling 'strategies for the next decade,' and 'charting a corporate course ahead,' blah blah blah—I found out that Andy had *shelved* my report, was dissing it left, right, and center. But that was nothing, comparatively. Over the weekend, he had commissioned a new report from a tedious guy in marketing who he plays squash with, a guy who knows absolutely nothing about the future of music!"

"I do remember that, of course I do."

"The Sony suits don't have the faintest idea about the future music scene. They're like a drummer who's a fraction of a second behind the actual beat. You know what I mean? They need some kind of corporate click track . . . People are still buying music, but increasingly they're going to be essentially *borrowing* it, not buying it. See this?" She pulled a paperback out of her bag, and showed him the cover: *The Future of Music*. "I think almost everything the authors say is correct." When she said, "I think almost everything the authors say is correct," she had an earnest, open look that touched him: he could see her as a teenager, arguing with Vanessa about God, or Mrs. Thatcher.

"Well, fine." He was engaged now, they were talking on the same level, eye-to-eye about business. "But how are you going to make any money from music if no one's buying it? I hate to say the familiar words—*revenue model.*"

"And I really like the idea of borrowing songs," she continued, for the moment ignoring his question, though he knew she would return to it in her meticulous, vigorous way, "because that's what we all *wanted* to do when we were young. What's the point of that huge box of moldy old LPs, half of which only have one decent song on them? The very minor works of Joan Armatrading . . . *Godspell*—remember you gave me that one, Dad, after Vanessa and I saw the film? But yeah, the business model is still unclear: How do you make money from borrowing? It's hardly worked out very well for the public libraries, has it?"

"I'd say you need two things: You need enough borrowers that the total sum of each small individual fee adds up to something substantial. Secondly, this means that they're going to be borrowers in name only. They are still actually purchasers, but they're paying so little that they'll think of themselves as borrowers. And then they keep on doing it, with each new song. It's a con trick, really."

"Yes, absolutely right—you actually have great experience! Hey, *you* could be involved with my venture, if you wanted to be."

"You're joking."

"Yes and no. No."

He was excited, flattered even. It was the first time she had asked for his advice or assistance in anything to do with her work. Mostly she just spoke at him, a fluent and incomprehensible code—click tracks, residuals, compression, A&R, mechanical license, and so on. (A code he had been stealthily cracking in recent years with the help of Google.) Surely he *could* be involved in some way? If only she didn't need money.

"And it's not money I'm after. Just to reassure you. I don't need *help*."

"I didn't think it was."

11

Again, as at Heathrow: he had the strange sensation that he was *trying* to be anxious about the situation, and that this was difficult because he was also on a rare adventure with his daughters. When had he last sat next to Helen on a train? No one had that kind of time anymore. And America was peculiar, more foreign than he had expected, it sharpened his senses. What a contradictory place: for every limitation, there was an expansion, for every frustration, an easement. The train was absurd, trundling along at barely sixty miles an hour. And Penn Station was a bloody embarrassment to a great capital city. To a great city, rather. But this journey was extraordinary . . . it had a pioneer feel—the enormous Hudson, with chunks of ice like broken pavement in the water; and the huge wealthy forests, the valley full of forts and power stations and opportunistic houses glooming on vast icy bluffs, the railway stations more like adventurers' huts than anything in Europe—barely manned outposts without proper platforms, and with outlandish names . . . Poughkeepsie, Yonkers, Schenectady; the train high above the ground, the big wheels polishing the rails, and the driver blowing that childishly dissonant horn. Why did he blow it so often? Maybe because he enjoyed it so much? Perhaps that childish harmonica sound, the crushed klaxon peal, reminded him of being a boy again? Reminded him of Christmas Day, of blowing a spitty mouth organ fresh from the box. But then at other times it sounded less like a harmonica than an animal's long cry from the prairie. And that sound, the big easy loiter of it, *was* America for him, though he couldn't say what "America" was, except that sound. He would, at the very least, see the kind of life Vanessa lived in the States, her *American life*.

"Tell me what you know about Josh," he asked. "I mean, in practical terms."

"Vanessa's kept quiet about him, hasn't she? I don't know if he teaches philosophy or works at a Starbucks. Or both. Actually, I do know. He writes about technology. For magazines and suchlike."

"I knew that, too. It doesn't seem enough of a job, to my mind. Josh is short for Joshua, I suppose?"

"Come on, Dad, what do *you* think? Of course it is. He is quite a bit younger than her."

"Ah, how very scandalous . . ."

"Well, it could be a problem."

"Said as if you want it to be a problem."

"Not at all."

To be fair, Helen did know about age differences. Before she married Tom, she had lived for three years with a man who seemed dangerously close to late middle age, though being in the music industry he didn't act like it—went around in jeans and trainers, even turned up at a wedding dressed like this, and had a very juvenile haircut. He collected bass guitars and, according to Helen, took twenty-four pills a day, bullshit supplements of one kind or another. Alan had fiercely distrusted him. He still took not one single pill regularly.

"I fancy a wander to the buffet. You want anything?"

Helen made it clear enough she would never eat or drink anything, except perhaps bottled water, from the Amtrak café car.

"Mainly I just want to kick all those doors open," he said, smiling.

•

Off he went, his black Oxfords ready for kicking. She saw again his slightly long sleeves, and how formally he was dressed. Good jacket, crisp dark trousers, white shirt. He was elegant, had the parched elegance of skinniness, like Charlie Watts—the same kind of narrow, compact miner's body, all sinew and tendons. Pulleys and wires, somehow. Strength in that body, endurance above all. But also a harder body than his spirit, which was generous, expansive in some ways. At the end of the carriage, he stopped, a bit theatrically, looked back at her, and then kicked the hard black pad at the base of the metal door, quite sharply, as if it were a football. Nothing happened. He looked like an aging mime artist (but weren't all the great mime artists aging? . . .). He'd missed. Another kick worked, and he disappeared into the next carriage.

She'd reached a point in her life when she wanted both her children and her father to stop aging. She needed him to stay in the same place, not fade away. She needed him to be ahead of her. Maybe this desire for stasis was the very definition of being middle-aged, though surely she wasn't quite that yet? But why didn't Tom fully feature in her picture, her frieze? It was always just her and the twins; even in her dismayingly frequent nightmares, when in her sleep she battled men with knives and jumped out of fiery hotel windows, Tom was curiously absent. Why? Because she'd spent her teenage years in a household with one parent, and felt that to be normal? It wasn't normal. She could see herself in the backseat of the warm car, her dress sticking to the seat, and her parents *in front of her*, where they belonged: Mummy in the passenger seat, holding a map or reading aloud from the newspaper, and Daddy driving, his hand on the steering wheel, the calm sweat on the back of his neck, and that funny habit he had of slightly adjusting the knee of his trouser leg after each gear change.

There was a young family on the other side of their carriage, a girl and a boy, unremarkable but beautiful in their juvenility. Helen couldn't keep her eyes off them. If she'd been entirely honest with her father, she would have said that her eagerness to leave Sony (apart from the important fact that the bastards at Sony didn't seem to want her any longer, or want her *enough*) had a lot to do with the children. She couldn't really bear the travel, the long hours talking crap with people who didn't have kids, or didn't care that *she* had. There were guys, always guys, who deliberately prolonged meetings, at exactly 6:30 p.m., so that they didn't have to go home; whereas by that time of the day she had a need to be with her children that was drainingly physical. Sometimes she wished she could have two long lives, one straight after the other—a full life devoted only to work, followed by a second full life, devoted only to being a parent. The combination of the two was so difficult.

Winter sunlight threw a white trembling dagger of illumination across her left hand with its adult veins and adult wedding ring, across her father's *New York Times*, then briefly bleached out the virtual solitaire she'd set up on her laptop. They were coming into Albany, slowing down, and outside there were the usual American urban scraps—a body shop; redbrick warehouses with smashed milky windows, their bricks daubed with the fat, dirty-white, risen-loaf lettering of graffiti artists; parking lots with new cars in orderly ranks; a flat-roofed mall; and a weirdly new high school. She wanted to go home. But the light, the light: she loved the clear, therapeutic blue of these American skies! *When skies are blue, we all feel the benefit* . . . one of the greatest, saddest songs ever written. Her father was returning, clumsily bearing a flimsy cardboard box. He seemed to have bought everything in the buffet: a bag of Doritos, a large coffee, a bottle of water, and some kind of *soi-disant* Danish. She could see it sugar-sweating inside its clear plastic wrap.

"You've gone native," she said. "How were the carriage doors?"

"My aim got better and better."

She closed the laptop, not eager for him to see how she was squandering her time.

"We're coming into Albany, so we don't have long now. Eat up! It looks revolting."

12

She had a broken arm. Vanessa came carefully down the steps of her house to greet them beside the cab, her right arm in a—*pine-green?*—cast. How could she not have told him?

As soon as he saw his elder daughter, Alan felt he couldn't say anything to her about her depression, and was filled with despair. He couldn't say anything to her. But she looked surprisingly good, had lost weight. Her dark hair, always beautiful, wasn't baked into that matronly bun she had affected in recent years. It was loose around her neck. She was wearing tight jeans, and there was something else: no glasses. Had she left them in the house, or did she now have contacts? Her sweet face. He kissed her, held her to him, and then, as she went to embrace her sister, he said, "What happened? With the arm?"

But Vanessa, in a very Vanessa-like way, was fussing with Helen about whether they had given a big enough tip to the cabdriver. "We gave plenty," he said, annoyed that this was how they would begin things. He pulled the bags from the cab's boot, and double-slapped the roof of the car, as he'd seen the bloke at JFK do it: a smack on the rump and the horse is quickly dispatched. Not so, the driver was examining some piece of paper and wasn't in a mood to hurry. "Why can't he bugger off?" Alan muttered. Vanessa was beginning to look a little fearful, as she did whenever she perceived any conflict, and especially the glint of her father's temper, and Helen, seeing this, picked up their bags and moved them all inside. It was caustically cold, anyway.

Vanessa's house was at the top of a gentle hill, near the college campus, on what seemed to be the more expensive fringes of Saratoga Springs. It was almost rural, certainly more rustic than he had expected. There was a lot of wild land around the house, dead patchy grass mostly covered with snow, huge bare maples. The place was charmingly run-down. Probably Victorian, covered in long horizontal strips of elephant-gray wood, with tall old windows he immediately thought of as maiden-aunt windows (the old loyal face glimpsed for a second behind the uneven glass, the blurred candle flame, the winter outside) and an ample front porch on which two white rocking chairs, icily disabled, gestured at warmer seasons. The stairs were rotting, with several nails coming out. Josh was no handyman, then. Give him half an hour with a good hammer.

Inside, the house was large, loose, original. He wanted to study the pictures on the walls (some fancy abstract stuff; an Indian with a turban against a beautiful washed-pink background), to look closely at the bright fabrics thrown over the sofa and over the very baby grand piano (not a surprise, that piano, given Vanessa's early devotion, but a surprise still), at the rugs and books— these last were piled absolutely everywhere, as if in exaggerated homage to "the life of the mind." He had an urge to be dismissive, vaguely vandalistic. Surely she hadn't read them all? But the place seemed comfortable and free, somehow, and he also admired that. This was her life, then! This was where she read her books, and wrote (or failed to write). And played the piano. Cathy and he used to laugh at the repetitious practice, the same wooden pieces day after day, Van's narrow back turned to the room, the Mozart and Burgmüller audible anywhere in the house, even in the upstairs bathroom.

He took a minute before going into the kitchen, where Helen

was talking, at speed and volume, and Vanessa was stirring something in a pot with her good arm. Helen sounded confident as ever, but Alan knew that she spoke loudly, more forcefully, when anxious, and he was fairly sure that Vanessa knew this, too. How tedious that everyone was so nervous.

"That looks uncomfortable, can't Helen do it for you? What happened to the arm?"

"I already offered, she won't let me."

He had a strong desire to touch Vanessa again. He and Helen had not embraced or even pecked each other on the cheek last night, when he turned up at her room. The BlackBerry partly to blame, of course.

"I fell down the steps you just walked up. Just before Christmas, on the first ice of what's feeling like a very long winter. The good news is, I get the cast off next week."

"*That's* what happened?"

Vanessa didn't reply, but briefly slowed her stirring and looked at her father, a glance of tenderness, of pity almost. For an uncanny instant things were turned upside down: for he was supposed to protect *her*, if need be, not the other way round . . .

"Well, look after it. Those planks are going to get loose, maybe that was what made you fall. The nails are coming out, I saw when I was walking in . . . I like the house, by the way! What you've done with it. But the maintenance must be a nightmare. The windows are all shot, for a start."

"Dad, it's been here for a hundred and twenty years, quite a long time for an American house. Tell me about New York—last night, the hotel, the trip up here: *everything*. What do you think?"

"Great scenery from the train. You'll have to explain to me exactly what this 'upstate' thing means. Are we 'upstate' now?" asked Alan.

"It's quite simple," said Vanessa. "Technically, it means New York State north of New York City—*up* the state, like *up*river. As opposed to *down*river. Actually, it's a bit more specific than that, and generally refers to northern New York State. Yes, where we are now."

"That Hudson sure is one amazing river," he added, with an attempted American twang.

"All American rivers make English ones look like piddling streams. I like that."

"Dad availed himself of the Amtrak café car, against my advice," said Helen. "He's now officially addicted to Doritos."

"Sensible man."

"New York was pretty crazy for me, as per usual." Helen looked very finished and urban, alongside Vanessa. "Silly meetings, large amounts of dreary business, buzz buzz buzz. I'm just extremely *tired*," she concluded, perhaps more flamboyantly than she'd intended to. Alan was about to mention what she'd told him on the train, about wanting out of Sony, but refrained. Perhaps she didn't want Vanessa to know.

"Then welcome, both of you weary ones," Vanessa said quietly, "to the world-famous Saratoga Springs Rest Cure. Now, some lunch."

"Where's Josh?" he asked.

"He's in New York—research for a piece. He won't be here till tomorrow. He sends apologies. He's very keen to meet you both. Of course, he's heard nothing whatsoever about you." That was more like the old Vanessa, whose sense of humor resembled her sister's, so that at the dinner table, years ago, if you had shut your eyes, you couldn't tell them apart—joke for joke, cruelty for cruelty, sweetness for sweetness, allied but apart. Now they sat at Vanessa's big pine table and had a late lunch. Through the drafty tall windows, the white landscape had a frigid glow. But the clouds were closing in. He watched his two highly intelligent, grown-up daughters, as they approached and drew back from each other, like switched magnets: Helen apparently more confident, acute, with her slightly sharp teeth, elegantly handsome, but also being disagreeable somehow, as if she were necessary medicine Vanessa just *had* to take; Vanessa quieter, softer, with her long dark hair and slightly squinting eyes, but exact, precise in her every word and thought, and so, to him at least, quite as formidable as her more obviously intimidating sister. How had he and Cathy produced them?

Helen was talking about Tom and the twins—Tom didn't really do his share around the house, she was so tired when she got home, she had so little time, and it was frustrating that the nanny hadn't tidied up or done the kids' dishes but was just *squatting* on the ground, as if her willingness to get down onto the same level as the kids absolved her of adult duties. Again, there was the blade of complaint, as if it were all his fault or more likely Vanessa's. In fact, Alan didn't care for Tom that much, was a little suspicious of him from the start, Tom quickly breaking one of his cardinal "male rules": he clapped his hands when someone told a joke or a funny story. (Everyone was now doing this, but men at least could refrain.) And Vanessa, deliberately refusing to provide the desired sympathy, was now slyly implying that Josh was a domestic paragon in this respect, a male feminist who did all the cooking and shopping. When it came to cleaning—"the historic feminist fault line," she said—neither of them cared too much about it: they muddled through. Of course, Vanessa conceded that unlike Helen, they didn't have children, so there was less mess, less work to do. Less of everything, thought Alan, with a tremor.

And then Helen, perhaps softened by Vanessa's concession, was asking her sister about her academic work, and Vanessa got that delicious look of frowning concentration she had whenever philosophy was at issue, her tongue unconsciously peeking out of her mouth. She explained that she'd recently been to a conference, and shyly suggested that part of the conference was devoted to a discussion of her old paper about marrying Anglo-American analytic philosophy with European theory, and how she delivered a kind of postscript to that original paper.

"I did a riff on the old joke about how the difference between them is that English analytic philosophy examines your moral obligation when you have an overdue library book, and European philosophy examines your moral obligation when the Nazis invade."

"When the Nazis invade, they'd close all the libraries and burn the books anyway," said Helen swiftly, as if solving the issue there and then. Vanessa smiled and looked at her father.

"That's *great* news about the conference," he said. "People were giving talks about your work?"

"Well, for two hours, between four and six on a Friday, after most people had gone home. It was a two-day thing."

"Come on, Van," said her sister, "admit a triumph."

Vanessa said nothing, looked full of color for a moment, and stood up, reaching for Helen's bowl.

"Look, let us do that," said Alan. "You've only got one bloody arm. Thank God it's your right one, though. Do you remember, *I'm left-handed, but—*"

"*But in my right mind*," finished Helen. "We remember."

"I always liked that joke, for some reason," he said.

"It's on a par with those others, Dad," said Vanessa.

"*My mother-in-law has been on the continent for a week . . . Well, has she tried bananas?* Your grandpa loved that."

"And, *The Commer has come to a full stop*," said Vanessa with childish enthusiasm.

"For years, I didn't get that one, and was too embarrassed to ask," said Helen. "And then I asked you and you explained that it was about Granddad's Commer van."

"Yes, his Commer van *was* always breaking down," said Vanessa.

"Astonishingly unreliable vehicle, even by British standards . . . By the way, do you still have your old NatWest bank account, in Newcastle?" Alan asked Vanessa.

"The one I opened at sixteen? Yes, I do. What a funny question, where did that come from?"

"I don't know, just thinking about your childhood, about old things, I suppose."

"I do still have it, and I even have some real British money in it," Vanessa added.

"Good."

"You mean 'good' as a deposit for my eventual return?"

"No, just good," he said.

"Good in itself?" She had the Querry tease in her face.

"Yes. You never know."

"Money in the bank," said Helen, doing a Durham accent—troublingly well. "Money in the bank" was what his own dad used to say to him. *Not much, but same an' all, it's money in the bank.* His father never knew that Alan got hold of his parents' bank account number, and secretly deposited small sums every so often, not large enough for them to notice, thirty or forty pounds only.

•

At the end of the summer holidays, not so long after her attempt to run away from school, Vanessa had gone with her father to open that bank account. Alan guiltily put four *hundred* pounds into it, as if that might help. Vanessa remembered well that large sum, and not being able to say anything about it. She couldn't thank him, even if she had felt like it, which she hadn't, particularly. She couldn't tell Helen, who had apparently not been granted the same largesse. It was the summer when the divorce was made final, became a legal fact. But her anger at that time wasn't about the divorce so much as the way Dad had acted earlier in the summer, when she had the job at the café in Corbridge and got close to a boy who worked there—called Alan, unfunnily enough, except that his name was spelled "Allen." Dad clearly couldn't stand the idea that she might be about to go out with a local boy who'd left school at sixteen and had a very "strong" Northumbrian accent, and he did everything he could to ensure that they did not spend much time together. "Okay, Van, you'll take this the wrong way, but I'm not sending you to a pricey boarding school so that you can marry a plasterer's son from Corbridge. He has no bloody prospects. None." He actually *said* that. She wouldn't believe it now, except that she'd always been a passionate diarist, and she had those words down on paper, dated August 22, 1982.

Allen Farnley was a lovely boy with a beautiful soul and a slightly coarse, heavy face. He looked older than sixteen, with bulky shoulders and long arms he held tightly down against his sides, like an owl at rest. He might have been "a plasterer's son," but he was at war with his semiliterate family. He knew a lot more than Vanessa did about classical music, kept Brahms and Ligeti scores under his bed. He was greedy for everything, for all knowledge, he swallowed the universe like a pill. That was a phrase they had discovered in an essay by Robert Louis Stevenson, discovered it together, it became the phrase of the summer of 1982: *swallow the universe like a pill.* Allen's dad was worried that his son was homosexual—*queer*—which was especially amusing to Vanessa, because he never stopped staring at her bum in the café, and eventually got his way. Not *all the way*, they were both too shy and inexperienced for that, but there was a breast squeeze or two, a lot of kissing, and she remembered an inexpert hand stolidly wedged between her legs as a kind of stabilizing device, the way chocks were wedged under the wheels of an aircraft: ecstasy always paralyzed Allen, it was the same when he listened to music. They talked a lot about God, and tried to "philosophize": What is music? What is "the good life"? Does death make life pointless? And so on. She had no idea where he was now. But she doubted that Allen's life had suddenly developed "prospects." Of course she was never going to marry Allen. They both knew there was no real future in it. Even at sixteen, she slightly pitied her father for his misplaced anxiety. She looked at him, across her own dining table. Here he was, at last: he had come all this way to see her in America. He looked tired. His handsome, narrow face was pale, and she realized that she could no longer picture him as a younger man. That loss tormented her whenever she thought about her late mother: she could still hear Cathy's young voice but could no longer *see* her as a young woman. Poor Dad, with his worries and all his striving, and his endless "northern" will! What was the point of that extraordinary will? To succeed, to make something, a successful company, to make money, to have children, to keep that beautiful old house . . . But he hadn't kept hold of his wife, and so he hadn't really managed to keep hold of his family—hadn't kept the family *intact*—so what good was the beautiful hollow old house? Now he was just old, like everyone else will eventually be, and soon enough he wouldn't possess the last remnants of any of it. You swallow the universe like a pill, but then you piss it out, too, it passes out of you, along with everything else important. Yes, she *must not think like this, must not dwell on things like this*—so everyone seemed to be telling her, so Josh told her, so Dr. Lasky hinted— but it was very hard not to.

Helen, she remembered, was patronizing; she implied that she found Allen Farnley hideous but that Vanessa couldn't really afford to be choosy. Vanessa was looking forward to Josh's return tomorrow, because Josh was undoubtedly handsome, was better-looking than Tom, and was younger, too. Helen's husband was beginning to wither on the vine, somewhat.

"Does anyone object if I have a smoke?" she asked.

"No, blow some of it my way," said Helen.

13

They left after lunch, and went to the hotel to check in. A cab was called, and it was the same driver who had brought them, the genial Muslim bloke who had asked them, on the way from the station, where they were from, and having discovered they were British, had picked up an enormous book from the front passenger seat and waved it: "You know Robert Fisk? The *British* journalist Fisk? He tells the truth, it's all there in his book." Alan had admired how smoothly Helen had handled him, and was looking forward to another display of her finesse. But he was on his phone, talking in Arabic, and ignored his passengers, who sat quietly and looked at the streets.

"Christ, it's bleak here," said Alan. It was getting dark quickly, and somehow the snow that had fallen the day before seemed already shabby. A massive orange truck, with a plow at the front, passed by and spat salt at them. You could taste the salt in the air, the snow was coming down as flakes of salt.

"It's really *not* bleak." Helen was shifting impatiently in the car, her face long and unappeased. "Saratoga is one of the nicest towns in America. If you want bleak, I can show you. Drive half an hour or so from here to Troy. Now *that's* bleak. Or at least it looks pretty bad from the highway. Troy seems almost Soviet—rotting old warehouses, dirty factories, there's a grim river, and horrible new blocks of buildings that look like hotels for the fat party apparatchiks . . ."

"All right, it's not bleak. But it's so bloody cold . . . Maybe, with the other place, its name laid a curse on it? What *were* they thinking? *Troy*, indeed . . ." The cab was moving slowly down an admittedly handsome main street, it was called Broadway, wider and more spacious than its English equivalent. The buildings were ornate, proud, redbrick or faced in stone. He was reminded of certain streets, still fine, in Newcastle or in Harrogate. The ones that got away, that escaped the bombers and the town planners . . . These eminent nineteenth-century American buildings stood like stone ghosts of lost prosperity, impotent but still accusing: we know what *we* did, what we achieved, but what have *you* built for the future, what have *you* achieved? Good lord, the Adirondack Trust Company, presumably a bank, looked like the Lincoln Memorial. It seemed to be made out of marble, with two huge Greek columns on either side of the main entrance. And almost next door, they were pulling up alongside it now, was an extraordinary building, their hotel, called the Alexandria, done up like a Venetian palazzo. There were three levels, with rows of tall, narrow arched windows. There was a piazza balcony on the first floor that ran the length of the building, with thin columns and filigree fretwork everywhere. He reckoned it was late nineteenth-century, though knowing this country it might easily have been authentic Renaissance, nicked from somewhere in Italy and brought over in bits on a boat.

"I think you'll like this place, Dad. At the very least it'll amuse you. It's American sui generis. You can check out anytime you like, but you can never leave."

The lobby was dark, full of polished mahogany and plum-hued velvet. It was also frantic with *objets*—the hysterical congestion of the bourgeois Victorian parlor: two tall fig trees in brass pots, peacock feathers in jars, oak standard lamps, two hideously religiose Tiffany lampshades (casting pools of sacred dusk), a closed grand piano, a prim chaise longue with scrolled arms, a huge staircase, and asylum-grade drapes, thick as prison walls, at the window frames. There was that cinnamon smell again. Dixieland jazz was playing through concealed speakers. The effect was archival, as if color were trying to turn itself into sepia and earn itself a caption: "Olde Saratoga." If he'd been less tired he'd have enjoyed the joke—except that it wasn't quite offered as comedy. He needed to call Candace, and sleep for a bit. Helen was back on her BlackBerry, ably prodding. The girl behind the registration desk did not inspire confidence; at her side was a plate with a vast, half-eaten piece of cake. She put her fork down and looked up. "Welcome to the Alexandria!"

But check-in was easy, and a few minutes later he was sitting on his hotel bed, the second in two days, and pulling his shoes off. The bedroom was less funereal than the lobby, but still ornate. He was sitting on a roofless four-poster bed (the four wooden columns made him think of the tie-rods that poke out of concrete foundations); there was another chaise longue, in striped pink-and-cream satin: at either end, the fat cylindrical cushions, buoyantly tight, were less like cushions than flotation devices. He looked directly onto the main street, with its fine shopfronts and ornate antique lamps.

Snow was now blowing in the air, illuminated in the arc of these lights, scurrying sideways and returning like large wet insect-clouds, white against the flat violet air. The window glass was appallingly cold on his forehead.

There was a knock at the door: "Room service." He hadn't ordered anything, and for an absurd James Bond second—him again!—Alan thought he could be in a film. It was a real hotel employee, and he was bringing the hotel's complimentary glass of champagne. Fairly bad champagne, it turned out, with a single bloated raspberry struggling to stay afloat.

He phoned through to Helen's room. "A bloke just came to give me a glass of champagne with a raspberry . . ."

"He just came by my room, too. They didn't *used* to do that." Helen had stayed twice at the Alexandria, both times in the summer, when the hotel's old-fashioned outdoor swimming pool was a necessary treat. She'd come up to hear Dave Matthews at the Performing Arts Center, one of the best places in America, she said, to hear live bands.

"I know what you're fishing for: okay, Vanessa seemed fine. To me. A bit limp. A bit damp. Do you know that 'damp' is an actual category in Chinese medicine? Too much 'dampness' is rectified with certain foul-smelling hot teas."

"When I think how close you were as kids, how Vanessa admires you and admires what you do . . ."

"Admires what I do? Pop music? I don't *think* so, Dad."

"Yes, she does. You don't know."

"The Philosopher and the Music Executive. It's an updated Aesop fable, with her as the wise old owl and me . . . as the foolish donkey or something."

"I don't think anyone would *ever* think of you as foolish," he said—admiringly, in spite of himself.

"As the greedy fox, then?"

"Oh, for God's sake, Helen . . ."

"Well, I thought she seemed okay. And to tell you the truth I couldn't see a sign of any particular new crisis. Maybe she seemed a bit nervous. And she *looked* quite good, different somehow, more done up. She's got contact lenses now."

"But the arm! So she really *did* fall. Josh wasn't exaggerating. It was serious."

"She slipped!"

"Why the hell didn't she tell us about it? Isn't that suspicious?"

"Maybe, maybe not. I think she likes the drama."

"That's unfair. You can't accuse her of enjoying the drama if she kept it a bloody secret! Find out for me? I need to know if it was an accident. *I* can't do it, Helen . . . I'd better call Candace now, then have a sleep before we regroup tonight."

14

C andace wasn't at home. He tried her on her mobile, but she was driving, and couldn't give her full attention to him. They spoke over each other, and managed to say, "No, go ahead," simultaneously. He'd never much liked making phone calls, maybe another reason he had not been a thrusting, *truly* successful businessman, those blokes in the movies with their feet up on the desk and the phone cradled lovingly like a pet lemur on the shoulder. His parents had always been atrocious on the phone, they came to it too late in their lives and treated it with humble respect, which annoyed him when he was older—this clinging atmosphere of modesty, as if the machine were only for emergencies, donated by the generous colliery bosses. Even now, though she had a telephone in her room, his mother tried to keep conversations short, would try to end them with, "Look, this is *your* call, it'll be getting pricey." (Since he was paying her bills, it was always his call, anyway.)

Candace, so far away, was tender but practical. She told him to have courage, but also advised him to look for certain "signs"— if she says she isn't reading anything, or isn't playing the piano, or doesn't want to get out of bed.

"Don't be ashamed to go through her drawers or bathroom cupboards to find out *exactly* what drugs she is taking. I wouldn't think twice about it." (Ah, the excellent Chinese steeliness.)

"What's puzzling is that she seems in fairly good spirits. I don't see any of those signs. She doesn't seem depressed. But the stairs: I was right! It *was* serious. She broke her arm and is wearing a cast."

"Love—depressed people don't necessarily go around with a big 'D' pinned to their chests. She broke her arm on the stairs?"

"Yes, and *said* that she merely slipped on the ice."

"Well, maybe she did really slip? Sometimes a cheap cigarette is just a cheap cigarette—the Chinese version of the Freudian saying, by the way."

"I wish you were here with me. Just you and me. I *know* you like hotel rooms . . ." He was lying on the bed, with most of his clothes off.

"You're breaking up on me, I can't quite hear you . . ."

"Seriously?"

"No," she laughed, "that was a joke, I can hear you fine. I can hear your words, and I can hear perfectly well *behind* your words, too." His daughters thought Candace was completely humorless, but in fact she had a zany, slightly unfunny sense of humor, which he adored.

"Your mother phoned yesterday. I think she was confused about your departure date. I gave her the hotel number. Though I bet she won't phone you long distance, in the States."

"You spoke to her?"

"You sound so terrified . . . It's one of those rare astronomical events, but it *is* physically possible."

"Sorry, it's just that you try to avoid her whenever possible."

"And she, me. Mutually Assured Avoidance."

Yes, that was true enough. He dreaded the idea of his mother coming to live with them.

"I think your acronym would be pronounced . . . 'Maa.' Where are you driving to, by the way?" He just wanted to keep her on the phone.

"I'm on my way back from the one-day course in Newcastle,

remember. 'The Feeling Buddha'? Part of the Zen Therapy foundation module."

"Ah. Good for you, my love."

Alan sometimes felt guilty about his resistance to Candace's Buddhism, but mostly he felt bullish. He was constituted by his desires. Certainly by his desire for Candace, which had brought sex roaring back into his existence after too many years of nothing. God, the tight creases behind her elbows when her arms hung down . . . Her slender back, her nice prim bum and those ridiculously small thongs she liked to wear, which in their lacy frailty were like dainty triangles strung on daisy chains, begging to be ripped off in a single erotic gesture, or quickly shoved aside at the crotch. Quickly pricked. If he got rid of desire, as his book on Zen Buddhism suggested, what would be left of him? Not a self, as he understood it. A driverless train, like the ones at Zurich Airport. She didn't know that he sometimes encouraged their Jack Russell terrier, on evening walks in the garden, to lift his leg and piss on the little stone Buddha who squatted on the grass next to the birdbath. Alan had nothing against the real Buddha, who was obviously a highly enlightened cove, but that stone bust in the garden, purchased by Candace on the Internet, was rather annoying. Come rain or shine, dry wind or spurt of yellow dog piss, the chubby little chap, an Asian Michelin Man inflated with nirvana, bore the same inane grin, his impassive smile an ideally mild weapon against desire, suffering, death, and war. He wasn't religious, had never been attracted to it, but what puzzled him was that Candace didn't seem very religious either. Perhaps Buddhism wasn't a religion in that sense? More power to it, then . . . His parents were fairly hostile to religion, good socialists that they were. Da would go every year to the Miners' Gala, but *not* to the religious service at the end of the day in the cathedral, with the brass bands from the county collieries, and everyone sucking up to those velvety deans and archdeacons, who were plummy with Christian consolation. Alan did like the cathedral, would occasionally slip into the massive, dark building without telling his parents. But as for the doctrinal stuff, it was obviously man-made nonsense. And as for the question of God—well, he had a notion that "the question of God" might all have been more or less *sorted out* in his lifetime, like Cyprus or polio. Vaguely, with lazy irritation, he imagined some final event or revelation, a kind of theological press conference. He didn't know whether the final revelation would be that God existed or didn't; what seemed strange, as he put his tired head down on the hotel pillow, was that it hadn't yet been *decided*, two thousand years after Christ's death.

15

Vanessa phoned, to propose that she come to them for dinner. The hotel food was uninspired—but it was so cold outside, and they could at least stay indoors. She would pay. Alan insisted that *he* would pay, and she crumbled with graceless, childish haste: "Oh, all right then."

They were waiting for her in the lobby when she arrived twenty minutes late. Helen, who had changed and looked furiously sleek in a tight black woolen dress, was of course beginning to get irritated, though they had drinks to sustain them. But Van had changed clothes, too. Alan assumed she was trying to keep up with Helen, but why would she want to? She had never shown the slightest inclination. When they were younger, Helen almost curated her many clothes—tended to the sartorial archives, kept a closet of perfectly ordered fashionability; dresses, skirts, nice jeans, and so many shoes, scrupulously aligned in rows, that Alan used to joke that her bedroom was like the antechamber to a mosque. But Van's clothes all seemed to be the same color—hues of gray and black—and were left in sour piles all over her bedroom. Clothes belonged in the same neglected, even disdained, category as television, exercise, and friends. Alan and Cathy hoped for more of all these things in Vanessa's life, and this minor-key anxiety became the reflexive mode of parenting. She needs more friends . . . She should go for a good walk . . . She should bike over to Corbridge . . . How can she meet someone *special*? . . . And now, after a couple of forgettable disappointments in love during her early thirties, she *had* met someone special—and Alan realized that of course the clothes, the improved hair, the contact lenses, were not for Helen, but for Josh. She looked radiant tonight, in a gray skirt and a sea-blue Indian top, inlaid with sequinny whatsits, and wearing a mother-of-pearl hairband (he had never before seen her wear a hairband). And her lovely eyes: he couldn't get used to the idea of her without spectacles.

It's not what I would have worn, thought Helen, but for Vanessa it's pretty good, especially the skirt. She felt warmer toward her sister when she looked better, when she had *made an effort*. Dear God, was she as shallow as that? Oh, she was weary: as she looked at Vanessa, she didn't know if she could do three days of this immense sisterly engagement. When Van had her "collapse," in her final year at Oxford, her father had asked Helen, who was in London, to go to Oxford and bring Vanessa home. Two nights on the freezing floor of Van's room at New College, and a day's train journey up to Northumberland—enough: unhappiness was so *boring*, in the end. She wanted the best for Van, of course she did, but she had her own very pressing concerns at work, and Tom had been such a shit to her just now on the phone, and she wanted to be home with the kids. Of all that, Vanessa knew next to nothing. She had never really asked Helen about her work, at Sony or before; she had met the twins exactly once. In London, two years ago, Van handed them each a hideous stuffed toy, ruffled Jack's hair (which made him cry), and then lapsed into wary watchfulness, as if she were keeping her eye on a dormant but largish spider. To be fair, it couldn't be said that she herself was much better with the babies in the early days: "latching on," for God's sake . . . Everything was difficult—the twins doubled all anxiety, all practical problems, doubled the terror. And doubled the joy, too. What did Van know about the joy of being a parent? This happiness was intensely private—she and Tom shared it, and didn't need to speak of it. Joy seemed so much more incommunicable than grief. Grief had tears, the visible signs, the obvious rain of sadness, and in that way was ultimately childish. Grief took you back to childhood, to the performance that got an adult running: "What's wrong, why are you crying?" But what was the sign of joy—the sun of joy? Who came running to the joyous one to say, "Why are you smiling? Tell me what makes you so happy?"

•

The dinner was proving uneventful, thought Alan. It was wrong to think of it like that, of course . . . Vanessa had spent a good part of the evening telling them about Josh. She had met him eight months ago, at a conference in Boston, on technology and consciousness. Vanessa was delivering a paper, Josh was poking around to see if there was something to write a piece about. He was only thirty-three, seven years younger than her, but had lived a few lives already, according to Vanessa's account. He started and abandoned a Ph.D. at Columbia; taught briefly in a very poor Brooklyn high school; wrote an unpublished novel (on his mother's old Corona, for the beatnik hell of it); and was now "figuring out what's next," while earning a perfectly decent income writing pieces about technology and innovation for magazines like *Wired* and *Rolling Stone*. To Alan, this sounded like a handful of snipped threads, and no pattern. It didn't matter how brilliant he was—Van said that he was the brightest person she'd ever met—if he didn't stick at anything. And Alan had other thoughts: it can't possibly be true about his earning a decent salary from freelance journalism. She's keeping him. As the financial benefactor, Van has the upper hand. But as the younger man, Josh has the upper hand. A bloke who won't stick at a job won't stick at a relationship. And how she loved him! That much was obvious. When Vanessa spoke about Josh, she was shy and alert at once, a beautiful combination. She sat up straight, and perched on the edge of her seat, and stopped eating.

There was a lovely cherry tree in the garden in Northumberland: in the spring, it shed so much blossom that the air around it seemed to be charged with pink activity. When they were small, the children would climb onto the lower branches, and jump off into that rouged carpet; the little kid-glove petals clung to their clothes when they stood up. Each time they jumped, even though he knew it was safe, even though he had been a thousand times more reckless when he was a boy—Alan and his best friend, William, used to race their brakeless bikes down Western Hill, and once he walked in his bare feet along the Elvet Bridge parapet—he tensed himself, prepared for disaster. Sentimental of him, and certainly not very useful: imagine if his own parents had been as soft and anxious . . . Still, he wanted that carpet of blossom to stay forever on the grass, he wanted his children only to jump from the lower branches. To see them grow older was to realize that they would only climb higher and higher, and that all he could do was silently watch, as they jumped.

16

The same night, at her desk, Vanessa was looking for an old diary, the one she had kept in 1982. She had a drawer full of personal scraps, and she often sat and sifted: it was better than reading a novel. She thought of it as her English drawer. There were many photographs; the program from her mother's funeral; old school reports ("Vanessa has been studying Juvenal's Tenth Satire with reasonable enthusiasm," wrote Miss Plummer); a road map of Northumberland; three love letters; a block of formal writing paper, engraved with the address of New College, Oxford; letters from her mother, including the first she received at Oxford ("this is the beginning of everything, darling—your first real step into adulthood; how envious I am that you are taking it while still so young"); a Pitkin Guide to Durham Cathedral—it had lost its back page; the driest note she ever received from a professor at Oxford, typed by the philosopher P. F. Strawson onto a white Magdalen College postcard and left in her box at New College, a note now astounding to her—certainly when compared to the cosseted American college scene—in its teasing and ironic discretion, its condescending respect, its willingness to treat a student like a feckless adult ("Am I right in thinking that you still have my little book about Kant? If so, perhaps you could leave it at the Magdalen porter's lodge for me—with any essays you have managed to write. I think you

owe me at least one. I hope you have recovered from your illness");
notes she made, at the age of twenty, on an essay by Thomas
Nagel; many letters from Helen; a guide to learning German;
blunt pencils and defunct staplers; a story she wrote when she
was ten years old ("I mount Arrow, my favourite horse, using the
stirrups, not the mounting block. Mummy and Daddy are watching me, and they are frouning—they are afraid I will fall off! I
click my heels and then we are off, into posting trot . . ."); her
InterRail Pass from 1983, and the all-important Thomas Cook
European Train Timetable; old student ID cards, not hers but
Helen's (1980s hair!—the Toyah Willcox week, the Suzi Quatro
season); ancient Rizla cigarette papers, unused but now so old
they looked smoked, burnt with age . . .

   She found the diary, and located the relevant passage. There
it was, and the words she had remembered were very close to the
original: "I couldn't believe that Daddy would say what he did
about Allen. That he would sit there and lecture me about love?!
'Van,' said Daddy, 'you won't like to hear this, but I'm not paying
for your expensive boarding school down south so that you can
marry a plasterer's son from Corbridge. It's not happening. His
family have no prospects.' How glad I am that I didn't tell
Mummy!" She read on for a line or two, and then in fascinated
dread began to flick through the pages, through weeks and months
of her old, old life, afraid to stop because if she stopped she would
have to read herself properly, afraid to find what she knew was
lurking there, in the same diary: "Happy today. But why?"

17

Up early the next morning, Alan had breakfast in his room. His promised "croissant," an obese horn of plenty, didn't deserve even its mispronounced name. But the coffee was excellent, the sun was melting the snow—it sounded as if a hundred old taps were leaking—and the American sky was joyfully, piercingly, utterly blue. He understood what Helen had meant when she told him to bring sunglasses. It was as bright as the Alps. They weren't due at Vanessa's until lunchtime, and Helen had work to do. Business. Alan, too. He was aware of having had a dream, now vague in content except for the general memory of horror, about the Dobson Arts Centre and Café. The waterfront—he'd had such hopes for it. But David and Lee were the wrong partners, he knew that, even five years ago; they did nothing to help. It had taken so long to get off the ground, the city hall people had been utterly obstructive, and the whole thing had swallowed the firm's resources. It was going to drag him down . . . That's what the dream had been about, being dragged down. He glanced at his little laptop, a proud white magic box full of secrets and tricks. Yes, he should check his e-mails, see what Eric Ball had to say about work back in Newcastle, but he couldn't really bear to open Pandora's box, he hadn't touched the thing since leaving Northumberland; so he decided to go for a walk, explore a little.

What had been snowily shrouded yesterday was sharp and bright now, each building immaculately lucid against the blue air. He walked along the main street, where plows had cleared a narrow path between firm, gritty walls of dead snow. What a baroque, and actually quite appealing, place it was . . . There was the Alexandria Hotel, of course, in its Venetian finery; and a big squat post office, a real art deco bulldog, whose doorframe of solid brass was adorned, he noticed, with undeniable gold swastikas; the marble pomp of the Adirondack Trust Company; a huge nineteenth-century apartment building that loomed over the street like a contested inheritance in a Victorian novel—who owned it, how many of its units were occupied, who on the city council wanted to tear it down? The upkeep on a place like that: you could see where it was being neglected. Not on the ground level, where a row of decent enough shops and cafés was doing good business, but above. Outside Uncommon Grounds, a coffee shop of course, a Lab sat in the snow, noble and indifferent. At the pharmacy next door, a woman in a white coat was poking with a long pole at the underside of the striped canvas awning, to get the snow to slide to the ground. People were clothed gigantically, polar clowns in vast boots and puffy glossy coats. He felt underdressed in his gray wool overcoat and black leather shoes; he also felt cold, so obviously they knew something he did not.

The town seemed prosperous. He passed a fine new bookshop, with an enormous American flag outside it, some kind of expensive gourmet food place, but then came a row of hard-luck tales: one shop was boarded up; another sold what looked like arts and crafts trash; and another, called Rasputin (with a sign sporting a crude drawing of the bearded Russian invincible), held some secondhand LPs. Helen could have bought up the entire stock of the little record shop and made the day of its gnarled owner—he presumed it was the owner—a man who was somewhat Rasputin-like himself, just fatter; probably about as old as

Alan, but he'd been round the existential block a few more times: lined, tired, he stood on the doorstep, wearing a leather jacket and patched jeans, and held a ragged cigarette, or perhaps joint, in a beringed paw. The man was friendly, like so many Americans, and said "Good morning," which no one did anymore in England. He passed a hat shop called Hatsational, and then another apartment building—this one was well maintained; a sign said that it was a former synagogue.

He liked that people were living in the middle of town; this was now rare in Britain, where high streets were occupied by the same large businesses—Boots, Tesco, Marks & Spencer—and everything was pedestrianized, the streets paved in the same cheap municipal bricks of sickly russet. The uniformity was tedious: Durham looked like York, and York like Chester, and Chester like Newcastle. The Krauts were partly to blame; once they'd bombed the old hearts out of Southampton and Canterbury and Coventry and the other cities, there wasn't anything to do with them but build big ugly shopping centers and multistory car parks. Which was what the Germans had done with *their* bombed towns—Hanover, Hamburg, Braunschweig, beautiful Heilbronn. But the town planners and the city councilmen of the 1960s were far more efficient than the Germans. Under the pretext of "modernization" and "progress," they widened medieval lanes for cars and knocked down entire streets of lovely old buildings. It was scandalous, what was done to Newcastle. That trumped-up crook T. Dan Smith, and bloody Wilfred Burns—they were the modern vandals. Eldon Square, which had to be one of the finest Georgian squares in Britain, demolished in the 1960s to make way for a new shopping center. And the Royal Arcade!—he remembered his dad taking him there. You went past the British Oak Insurance Company, and into a magical, glass-roofed Victorian palace, with shops and offices. The glass of the delicate roof was always grimy-green. The Socialist

Hall and Café was at the back of the arcade, and was run by a strange red-haired man—Archie? Arthur?—whose voice had never properly broken. He wasn't a eunuch, he just had a high voice like a little boy's, even though he was at least fifty. Alan was embarrassed by him and wanted to turn away, but Da treated him normally. How did he manage to shout effectively at the waiters and cooks, with that little squeaky voice? The same crooked gang from the 1960s demolished that lovely old Royal Arcade, demolished the Socialist Hall and Café—for a round-about! Just knocked it down, so that Ford Cortinas and Triumph Heralds could zip in and out of the city. Don't blame the Germans. We did it to ourselves. The Europeans hadn't succumbed to the vandalism and mediocrity in the same way. They understood that a fifteenth-century town hall, a medieval corn exchange, a glassy Victorian arcade, were valuable in themselves. He went on holiday to these fine provincial towns, to Laon or Château-Thierry, to Ghent or Leiden (where, in the Protestant church, Alan marveled at the proud seventeenth-century statement, in gold lettering: *God Is Wonderlick*), and saw that the past was properly respected. The Americans shared some of that decency: they left the past alone, let it rot, if need be. Not necessarily because they respected the past—everyone always said they didn't, couldn't afford to, as New Worlders—but because they were care-less, individual, and had a bloody lot of space.

It was difficult for him to think about these things without some guilt. He had profited from what dismayed him. In New-castle, he'd been an early investor in the new commercial devel-opment of the quayside, and although most of the old buildings there had been unoccupied and undistinguished, he was some-times a bit wistful about the handsome redbrick Victorian ware-house that was knocked down to make way for the proposed Dobson project, in which Querry Holdings was one of three partners. In Durham, his firm developed the Flambard Houses, a decent but aesthetically mediocre block of flats on the site of a shabby terrace of half-timbered Elizabethan houses, owned by the university, which had stood in the same place unmolested for four hundred years. (The university had been embarrassingly eager to sell that terrace and turn a profit, he now recalled.)

That old cartoon—a man saying to a coworker: "I'd rather be a huge part of the problem than a tiny part of the solution." Eric Ball, who had started working for Alan fifteen years ago, stuck that cartoon on the door of his office (along with a name tag from a conference he had attended in Stuttgart, which read: "Herr Ball"; both men found it much more amusing than anyone else did in the office). The cartoon was funny. But what *was* the solution? Of course, growth was the problem and growth was the only solution. All modern economies were based on the desirability of growth. Cities naturally expanded and changed. And yes, sometimes those perfect little European towns felt murderously stifling; like those atrocious villages in the Cotswolds, where nothing has changed in six hundred years and the genteel inhabitants live like cupboarded gnomes of history, in tiny thatched cottages . . .

His whole life had been about change, growth, social mobility. In truth, he'd always been a bit wary of the Socialist Hall and Café. The seats there were communal wooden pews, and the thin men sat next to each other, and they all looked the same to him. They sat at their tea and bread and butter (Alan was wondrously allowed a stotty cake), with the same studious poverty, wearing the same flat caps, their faces pale as string, patient, humorous, modest—and finally conservative. Even the cocky ones wanted things to stay more or less the same: the dirty smoky gray mesh of the air, the defeated food and weak heaters, the dripping toilets full of old yellow bus tickets. Yes, the radicals—the leftists, the Communists—wanted more jobs and more money for everyone. And less money for the rich: redistribution. But as

Alan saw it, they wanted more money and jobs so that the smoky underlit impotent monotony of things could continue just the same as before. Da loved it all, made his way round the tables, shaking hands and chatting to people he knew from Swan Hunters and Parsons. Later, he'd go home and happily shut himself in the bedroom and write a rhyming poem—Geordie doggerel—about his "day in Newcastle" . . . (Da became something of a "poet" in his retirement.) But little Alan didn't know what to do, so he put his hands in his gray shorts, and studied the posters: "The 'Ascot' of Greyhound Racing: Every Wednesday and Friday Evening." And next to it: "This Saturday—Special Game—Newcastle United vs. Sunderland AFC." Little Alan looked around him and even then he knew this wouldn't be his world, not exactly, whatever his loyalties to his parents. He had to get away, had to leave it behind. He hadn't voted for Mrs. Thatcher in 1979, but he supported her during the miners' strike, despite the sometimes bitter arguments with Vanessa and Helen. For one simple reason: because Arthur Scargill said that as the miners' union leader, he was fighting for the right of his son and grandson to continue to go down the pit and hack away at coal seams. Who on earth wanted his own son to go down the pit just because *he* had? Why was it a right? It was a horrible, filthy, poisonous way to earn a living wage, and if you could extract the same coal by open-cast mining, without sending men down in cages like human canaries, then that was progress—even if two hundred of them were suddenly out of a job. In the north, thought Alan, as he made his way along Broadway back to the Alexandria Hotel, certain kinds of men wanted a history that was biblical, a timeless generation, of identical linked *begat*s—Dennis begat William, who begat George, who begat Colin, who begat Arthur, who begat Fred, all of them doing exactly the same as his pale-as-string ancestor. But Alan was proud that his grandfather had been a miner, while his father had risen—yes, risen *up*, out of the bloody ground—to become a ship's engineer and then to become the owner of a big shop in Durham, and that he himself had risen to become a property developer who drove a big Audi. David begat George, and George begat Alan, and Alan begat Helen and Vanessa. That was the march of generations, because something had actually been generated. Growth, in a word.

18

When they arrived for lunch at the gray clapboard house up on the hill, Vanessa was bright-eyed, restless. Josh was about to arrive, but his train from New York was delayed. Vanessa jumped up to put some music on, returned to the CD player to fiddle with the volume, moved her father and sister out of the kitchen to the sitting room, brought them drinks—warming tea for Alan, an irresponsible gin and tonic for Helen—and said twice, "I really wanted him to be here to greet you. I'm sorry he's late." Something garlic-laden was cooking; the smell, combined with the ingrained scent of tobacco, so familiar and familial, made Alan want to fall asleep on the sofa. Helen wondered if Josh really did do most of the cooking, as Vanessa had boasted.

She disobeyed her sister's orders and went into the kitchen. Vanessa was sitting at the table. Her eyes were closed and she was taking measured breaths, with her arms stretched out on the table, palms turned nearly upward, the green cast on the right arm resting heavily.

"It's a calming exercise I've recently learned."

"From a new therapist?"

"From the Internet."

Helen laughed. "That's a relief, because you look alarmingly like Candace on her Zen cushion, and I can't have two of those in the family. You mean that doesn't do the trick?" She gestured at a "Keep Calm and Philosophize On" poster that had obscurely annoyed her when she first saw it yesterday.

"Not even close," said Vanessa. "That thing's an incitement to chaos and insanity—I want to attack it every time I catch sight of it. But a colleague gave it to me. So . . ."

"Speaking of calm, I think Dad is so loving being looked after by the two of us that he's settling down for a nice long sleep on the sofa."

Vanessa stood up, walked to the stove, and checked a pot. Helen appraised her—critically (she was slouching, as usual), then helplessly—and the entirety of their childhood seemed to be tantalizingly present, she could see everything at once: those long summer days in Northumberland, when there was nothing to do except walk with her sister and the dogs, out on the hills and in the woods; afternoons lying on the bed together trying to speak more than three words in "burp language," or sitting in front of the television for *Blue Peter* and eagerly writing down "London W12 8QT" on a piece of paper. There was that argument about Granny's necklace, and all the new music they shared together (Van used Helen to bring the news about bands and records); Mum and Dad quarreling; and the sheep up on the high hills near the old house; and milk dripping noisily from Vanessa's spoon as she ate her cereal at breakfast, and Vanessa once calling Helen a "cunt." She could see it all, including coming up behind her sister and hugging her, which Van had never liked; and seeing all of this, as if concentrated in the lens of a single water drop, she wanted to burst into tears, and had to fight hard to control herself. What silliness, stupid silliness!

To help with her own rescue, she asked, "How does Dad seem? To you."

"I'm so glad he's come," she said gently, which annoyed Helen on several levels. After a silence: "He's his old self, I guess."

"Which is?"

"Kind, self-contained, a bit detached."

"Never quite as detached as you think. Why do you think he's here, if he's so detached?"

"It's the only way he can get to spend four whole days with you," said Vanessa, perhaps seriously.

"It's not a competition, is it? I mean—only if you make it one." Vanessa said nothing, and kept her back to Helen. She was fiddling at the stove. Something about that turned back, the solid silent stubborn uncheerful wall of it, enraged Helen. She leapt up from her chair and grabbed her sister. "Please, please don't start this! Not while we're together." She struggled to keep her voice low.

"Start what? I was joking," she said. "Anyway, you can talk," she added, turning away from Helen. "Whatever I might 'start' was begun a long time ago by—other people."

Helen refrained from saying anything—what was the point of swimming in all this stale water? She wanted out, she wanted to go home, to lie next to the twins on their delicious little beds . . . Maybe Vanessa felt something similar, because she appeared somewhat ashamed: as she should. Of course Alan had heard, and was stirring, now walking down the corridor. He stood in the doorway in his socks, his white shirt cuffs undone—slight, strong, old.

"You know, you both look like grown-up women to me, you do grown-up things, so why you should act like teenagers is a mystery." He put an upright finger to his mouth, and then said: "Let's have no more." In an unconvincing attempt to divert attention, he pointed at the large carton of milk on the counter.

"Why are things so huge in this country? My croissant at breakfast was enormous. Like a snake had eaten a pillow . . . And that must be half a *gallon* of milk right there."

"I'm quite used to it. I like it," said Vanessa. "It's helpful when it comes to things like milk or detergent. And the fact that the carton is double the size doesn't make the contents half as good, you know."

"Not true. That was exactly the case with the croissant," said Helen, with her usual briskness. "Twice as big, half as good. I had the same breakfast as you, Dad."

"Okay, okay, let's not argue about it, I only brought it up to change the subject! I spent the morning walking around. You live in an interesting town, Van. Many great things—Broadway, is that the name? The main street. That old synagogue, the smart buildings right up against the crumbling ones, that fantastic old Victorian arcade . . ."

"Sometimes, all I can see on Broadway are the dead from the nineteenth century, taking their promenades, with their parasols raised. It's a slightly mournful place in that sense," said Vanessa. They both looked at her to see if she was joking; she was too obviously playing the role of the melancholic, the sensitive depressive.

"*I see dead people,*" said Helen breathily.

Alan quickly added: "And these weird American churches everywhere—I like the First Baptist Church. You wouldn't want to be a mere member of the Second or Third Baptist Church, would you?"

"Oh, Dad."

"Well, I'm just saying . . . Also, the vicar of the First Baptist, or whatever they call him, seems to have his own dedicated parking space outside the church, like a CEO. *Thou Shalt Not Park Here.*"

"Did the sign actually say that, or are you making another joke?" asked Helen.

"It actually said that"—though Alan had something light in his eyes which seemed to dare them to challenge him.

"Josh is here!" said Vanessa loudly, a second before the front door began to open.

He put down his shoulder bag, took off his coat, and walked

quickly, almost ran, to the kitchen. Josh was tall, lean, large-headed (though it was hard to be sure, because he had so much dark hair). He seemed flagrantly younger than anyone else in the room, the effect partly produced by his loose slenderness, and by his clothes—sneakers, old jeans, a gray T-shirt that read: I HAVE A SECRET PLAN. Vanessa tugged at him with her good arm, and leaned up for a kiss that continued for a second longer than was comfortable for her witnesses. Introductions were made. Josh was charming—or at least making some effort to charm—and was sweetly exuberant. He surrounded them with questions, wanted to know what they thought of Saratoga, of New York State, of the house, offered more drinks. He had gifts for Alan and Helen.

"Where did you find this?" said Alan with wonderment, as he opened his present—an old map, from the 1930s or '40s, of Northumberland.

"New York contains multitudes," said Josh. For Helen, he'd found a weird ragged book from 1976—really a pamphlet or chapbook—of poems and lyrics by Lou Reed. (Van had told him how much Helen adored Lou Reed.) He announced with satisfaction that only four hundred copies of this book were ever published.

He was young, and really *quite* good-looking, Helen thought. In the way of childless adults, he seemed like a visitor from a freer, more irresponsible land. Vanessa now had a sated, happy-doomed look on her face, a cat drowning in cream. Helen furtively studied Josh, trying to isolate what made him endearing. His nose was large, and she liked large noses, like her father's. Handsome eyes, expressive and tender, in sockets that sloped downward in an unusual way. Interesting dark eyes, which looked somehow seductively *guilty*. That was the word that came to mind. As Josh spoke, she realized that he lisped on his *r*'s and *s*'s, the tongue slightly too big for the mouth—a bird too large for its nest, a teenage boy whose feet have outgrown his socks. It made him seem

almost English; the English seemed to specialize in such defor-
mities, while Americans, she thought, rarely lisped in this way.
And because it made him seem English, it was neutralized as a
flaw, and made him seem more appealing still . . .

At lunch, everyone but Josh had wine; he swigged coffee
from a huge Skidmore College mug, which surprised Alan. They
spoke a bit about Saratoga, though the Querrys were now keen to
leave a subject they had been clinging to only for safety's sake.
Josh, unaware that the topic had been run dead the day before, assumed command. He spoke a little too loudly, thought Alan.
Did they know that the town was featured in James Bond, in
Diamonds Are Forever? Alan did. Did they know the story of
Solomon Northup, the free African American who was playing
the fiddle in various hotels around here, but who was kidnapped
on the main street, tricked into slavery, and then spent twelve
years as a captive in Louisiana? Helen knew about it; Alan, in
his morning walk, had seen a sign on Broadway commemorat-
ing that awful tale.

"And you know that Saratoga is the site of a famous British
defeat?" asked Josh playfully, but for some reason aiming his
question at Alan alone. "General John Burgoyne and the British
troops had what you would call their *arses* handed to them in
September 1777. Turned the tide of the Revolutionary War."

"I heard something like that at school, a long time ago. That
must be why there are so many bloody American flags up and
down your main street."

"You bet . . . Go, Americans! It's pathetic, right? Civic life as
an endless sports game, and anyone who dissents from the mindless cheerleading gets kicked out of the stadium. It's gotten much
worse since 9/11 . . . A writer I like has this great joke about how
if America ever gets a dictator, his national nickname won't be
Big Brother or Dear Leader, it'll be Coach."

"Josh really hates George W. Bush," added Vanessa, with a
reverence that slightly shocked Helen and Alan.

"I hope you do, too," said Helen to her sister.

"Oh sure, of course," she replied, distractedly. "Now, eat up."

"What I find hard to understand," said Alan, "is how this well-born posh bloke conned ordinary Americans into thinking he's one of them—a man of the people. I don't like the class system we have in Britain, but it has a few uses: we'd have seen through the lying. His fake accent would have given him away. It would've been like Prince Charles pretending to be a Cockney."

"Though if you stop to think about it," said Josh rapidly, almost casually, as if Alan's comment had indeed taken very little time to think about, "of course he *is* a man of the people. He's a lot like them because he shares their stupidity and ignorance. The public recognizes him as, like, one of its own."

"Is there in fact a single intelligent politician in America?" asked Alan. Josh chose not to rise to this, and merely gave him a glance of easy comprehension.

"Um, how about Senator Obama? Better than any British politician I can think of," said Vanessa.

"And I dearly hope he's going to be our next president," said Josh. The senator from Illinois had just announced his candidacy.

"He'll have plenty of repairing to do," said Vanessa.

Helen suggested that her father was quite patriotic, but in a modest way.

"That's not true. I don't believe in patriotism, just the opposite. I had a history teacher who convinced us kids that patriotism and nationalism were the reasons for most of the ills of history. It wasn't very hard to be convinced! He banged into us Samuel Johnson's line about how pat—"

"—patriotism is the last refuge of a scoundrel," finished Josh.

"So you know it, too," said Alan.

"Was that the 'England was in a mess' teacher?" asked Vanessa, coaxingly.

"Mr. Watson. Clag . . . that was his nickname." Alan turned slightly to Josh, who had finished his plate well before anyone else. "He came into the classroom one day, and he threw the contents of his desk onto his table, then he upended the waste-paper basket onto the table. Then he stood behind this huge messy mound, and declaimed—he was very theatrical—'In 1387, England was in a mess!' I've never forgotten that—how could I?"

"Was it 1387? Or 1487? Or maybe it was 1660?" asked Helen wickedly.

"Well, that's the bit I *have* forgotten. You see, I always say 1387, but the thing is, I can't remember the exact date."

"When was this? During the war?" asked Josh.

"Just after it. 1947 or '48."

"So he was really talking about Britain after the war. That's the 'mess' he was referring to."

"Yes, I suppose so." Alan was silent; he looked down, fiddled with his watch.

Josh was not unaware that he might be irritating Alan. He had been told, often but not exclusively by women, beginning with his mother, that his restless rapidity in conversation had a tendency to alienate people, who might mistake his quick passing for competitive sports. Try to show that you're on the same team as them, not on the other side. That was the essence. Be a bit gentler, slower, listen more. Josh took it to mean: Even if you can see three moves ahead, act as if you can't. The oil of duplicity that greases the social machine. One of the things he loved about Vanessa was that she didn't try to correct his behavior, in fact matched his speed with her own (a different style of rapidity, quieter, more internal, but ruthless when necessity called).

"It must have been difficult, growing up during the war—and afterward, too," Josh said. Helen saw that to improve the slight lisp, he sometimes made an awkward shift with his lower jaw, like someone wiggling a key in a reliably stiff lock.

Was it difficult? He was so young then, he remembered very little.

"I had a happy childhood. My parents protected me from a lot, I think. Kids have a harder time now. I wouldn't want to be a twenty-year-old in today's climate. We had real prospects after the war, though the economy was a shambles and rationing seemed to go on forever. At least we *felt* we had prospects. Actually, it was the late fifties by the time I started working, and everything *was* opening out by then. There was a National Health Service and a Welfare State, for one thing. That was a big difference from my childhood . . . People could suddenly get their teeth fixed. When I was a kid, it wasn't strange to see boys wearing their big sisters' coats, the day after their sisters had gone out wearing them. Everything was still expanding. And we still made things! Do you know who was the world's biggest exporter of cars in 1950? Great Britain. Now all the big British car companies are owned by foreigners."

"But it's a different global economy now," said Josh. "Yes? Innovation rather than replication. Ford's law—churning out millions of identical Model Ts—has given way to Moore's law." Alan wanted to reply, but didn't know what Josh was talking about when he said "Moore's law." Perhaps the lad was trying to be kind in his way?

"We owned a Jensen Interceptor in the 1970s," said Helen, with a show of irrelevance. "Hello, I can tell from your face that you don't know what I'm talking about," turning to Josh. "It was the most beautiful British sports car."

"Broke down a lot," added Alan. "Sir Matt Busby had one, and Lord Carrington."

"And John Bonham," said Helen.

"And then Helen ruined it all by naming her first band Jensen and the Interceptors. I couldn't take the beautiful sports car very seriously after that," said Vanessa, smiling a little wildly.

"It's not as if I took the band very seriously either. Remember cute Julian Vereker? The refusenik drummer?"

"I remember."

Helen was beginning to relax. They might all get along. Josh could be a bit intense, and she wasn't sure how Dad felt about him. But if she remained vigilant, she could probably keep them all happy. She did that kind of thing at work the whole time, a daily arena—the University of Hard Fucking Knocks—that soft Josh and lucky Vanessa never really had to set foot in. Josh wasn't the problem, anyway. It was Vanessa who was loose, a liability: look how that attempt to talk to her about Dad had been chewed up and spat back at her. Helen was enjoying a measure of righteous grievance when Vanessa, who was one-handedly clearing plates from the table, stumbled slightly and dropped a small celadon-green bowl. It hit Josh's plate, and a tiny piece of the bowl's delicate rim jumped into Helen's lap. "I have it," she said, and carefully put her fingers around its parched new edges.

Vanessa stood still, and lamented, "My favorite bowl! The *only* one I cared about."

Josh said that they could easily fix it; Alan added that she wouldn't be able to see the crack. Helen, rubbing her fingers along the chalky shard, rather enjoyed the trivial torment.

"You don't understand. It's not the bowl. Of course I can go to the potter who made it and get another one—he lives nearby. It's the idea: everything that is most dear to you will eventually be taken from you."

"Then that's a very important lesson to learn," said Helen, without emotion.

"Fuck it, leave me alone," replied Vanessa.

"All right, I'm going for a little walk," said Alan, who took his coat and woolen cap, and almost ran for the door.

19

He wished he still smoked. He was breathing out volumes of steam, but the act wasn't as satisfying as exhaling tobacco smoke. It was very cold, the air was thin, stilled; in the late afternoon light, everything had an atmosphere of earnest preparation for the long, bitter night ahead. Alan saw for the first time that Vanessa had a real view—of fields, and on the declining horizon a family of hills, bluish or bluish-pink in the twilight. They beckoned, as hills always had: How could you not want to go to them? They rose up like aspiration itself. He was a northerner, of course he loved hills. He once filled in a business questionnaire whose last query was "Name your ideal journey." To which he had replied, "Driving north." It had been initially amusing that Cathy, on a whim, had answered the same question, "Taking a train south." He must ask Van what those hills were called . . . He and Cathy were twenty-two when they met, and were married a year later. Alan was naively, vulnerably infatuated. You never loved in the same way again. She was tall, embarrassingly even a little taller than him, "middle class," and did that thing with her hair, layering a long plait, which he'd never seen any other woman do.

Behind him, the door opened, and he heard a careful descent of the wooden stairs, and then the unbearable dry squeaking of footsteps on packed snow.

"You didn't get very far," said Vanessa.

"Too bloody cold."

Still, they were walking away from the house. He was anxious that they would now have to have *the conversation*, and was glad that the deep cold would enforce a short exchange.

"You know I was mainly joking about the bowl? Appearances to the contrary."

"Ah, Van—now you'll tell me that Helen was also joking when she provoked you to swear at her?"

"No, I don't think *she* was, alas."

"Look, I'm very simple, compared to you and Helen." He had spent his life alongside melancholy and very complex women, beginning with his depressive grandmother: he could never *say* this aloud, of course. "Sometimes I get very tired, trying to be the one member of this family who is never 'unhappy.' Maybe this doesn't look like it takes any effort. You just chalk it up to my buoyant temperament—'It's Dad, he's like that, he's naturally fairly cheerful and optimistic.' But I'm not buoyant like a boat is, without any effort. I'm buoyant like a human being is. I have to work at it the whole time, or I'll sink in the water."

"I'm sorry, you didn't need to come here to keep *me* afloat."

"That's *not* why I'm here. That's not what I meant. I'm glad to be here, I've never seen where you live."

"And what do you think?"

"About Josh?"

Vanessa laughed with pride. "I didn't *just* mean Josh. But sure, start with him."

Alan paused. He had the sense of being ever so slightly indulged by Josh, treated as the old geezer from a superseded generation, whitely ex officio.

"Tell me about him."

"Daddy, you'll love him! Yes, he's earnest and intense and maybe a bit competitive. Jewish-confrontational. He likes to show off. Male stuff, peacockery. His father's a Chicago lawyer and his mum is a psychiatrist. He has two younger brothers. As far as I can tell, their family life was like a perpetual court trial—statements for the defense, statements for the prosecution, nightly convictions at the dinner table. The three brothers had to talk about a randomly chosen subject for ten minutes, fluently, without running out of steam. That was the family game. That produces a certain kind of young man, I guess. But he's not just super-intelligent. He's the most moral, kindhearted, most fundamentally decent person you will meet."

He loved that she said "Daddy." Pure balm. He discounted all the superlatives—they came with the romantic territory. But with what respect she spoke of Josh's fancy family! "That was the family game." The Querrys couldn't compete with *that*. What was their family game? Monopoly and anger? Scrabble and quarrels? Watching Bruce Forsyth's *Generation Game* on TV on Saturday nights? Alan was going to be a lawyer, and started studying law at university—but the real world was too attractive.

"He's certainly a good-looking fellow. Anyway, I've only just met him. You're very fond of him, that's obvious."

"Yes, Dad, I'm very *fond of him* indeed."

"Here, let's not get too far from the house—I don't fancy a long walk back. By the way, those hills you can see from the house, on the far horizon, that great pinkish color they had a few minutes ago. Do they have a name?"

"Of course. The Adirondacks."

"Ah, like the train."

"Like the hills."

"Can I ask you a question?"

"Sounds ominous." She was always alarmed, as a kid, when adults began an inquisition with "I've got a bone to pick with you." It was so palpable—two birds tearing at flesh.

"Does Josh actually live with you? I know that sounds strange. It's just that there's . . . no sign of his stuff or taste anywhere. It's all *you—your* books, music, paintings, posters." That's why he liked it so much.

"Well, how would you know which are my paintings and books? You'd be comparing them with your last visit? I'm sorry to be sharp with you, Daddy, but why are you playing the detective?"

He didn't say: because I was summoned here to find things out.

"You're right enough, I should have come here years ago . . . But I *like* that you always come to me in the summer, to Northumberland. It makes the house seem full again . . . Look, I suppose I was thrown by the fact that Josh wasn't there when we arrived yesterday. And then your house—in a good way—seems to be so much your place."

"It's a reasonable question, I'm sorry I took it the wrong way . . . Josh has a light footprint. He doesn't believe in accumulating things. So yes, the house is largely *mine*, whatever that means when I only rent the place anyway. Also he travels a fair amount for his work. You know all about that. We like it that way."

The self-righteousness of "light footprint." Why did Josh have to travel very much for his "work"? Most of what Josh did could be performed sitting at a desk in his dressing gown, one hand on the willing laptop and the other on his semi-tumescent dick.

"Well, good," he said.

"Yes, *good.*"

In despair at how poorly he was managing things, and with a little surge of punishment, he added: "Josh and Helen have been worried about you, but it seems there's nothing much to worry about. According to you." He was trying not to shiver; his body was rigid with effort.

"Of course Josh has been anxious, he's very compassionate. I haven't been sleeping at all well, and when you don't sleep, when you're awake all night, you have all kinds of 'bad thoughts.' The old demons . . ." She sighed. "I . . . what happens is that I go to bed with a piece of music in my brain, and instead of soothing me, this music repeats itself in an endless loop in my head, it becomes a kind of torture—like how the Americans are using music as torture at Guantánamo, though they use Britney Spears or Metallica or whatever, while mine is a bit of Schubert or a Bill Evans riff. It's highly unpleasant, is all I can say—it's awful, really. But things have been a bit better since Christmas. Well, since I broke my arm, in fact."

"And when you're tired, you can't function properly, and sleeplessness causes depression. That's well known." He wanted to be helpful, to be practical, above all. The comparison with Guantánamo seemed histrionic.

"If you haven't experienced true insomnia, you have no idea! I broke my arm because I could barely see straight, I was so tired. I slipped on stairs I've been up and down for three years. But the odd thing is that two weeks before I broke my arm, it stopped working properly, almost as if my body *knew* I was going to break it."

"Stopped working?"

"I had terrible pains from my elbow to my wrist, and it felt so heavy I could barely lift it."

"Look, in fact I've also had some periods of insomnia, and I did find, eventually, after a lot of searching around and some experimenting with different techniques, that *one thing* really helped. The right pillow—a nice hard one, and hypoallergenic. Mine was made by Laura Ashley, I don't know if you could get that brand in America." He knew he was clinging to a diversion, but didn't know how to proceed.

There was a sound from far away, an irregular pounding, the bigfoot tread of a large diesel engine, and then the noise began to swell, and suddenly it burst out like water, as if a deep river were flowing past them, very near, a huge river overflowing a valley, threshing and beating.

"Where's *that*?" He said it with delight.

"Right down there, in the valley. About five hundred yards from where we're standing. That's not a passenger train, by the way, it's freight. It's all cargo from now until tomorrow. There's a wonderfully long train I often hear at about three in the morning."

"I hope he blows the whistle," he said, like a child. "I love that whistle." Vanessa smiled at him, a smile of helpless affection, which he couldn't see in the twilight. And the driver did blow the whistle, the big American horn—it moaned across the valley, plaintive and glad at once. The harmonica, the klaxon, the crushed notes again . . .

As they approached the house, two darkish adult shapes, accompanied by a lawless and panting dog, crunched their way toward them. The shapes slowly gained definition: the man was round, the woman was thin; both were swaddled in layers of fat, shiny nylon—what Alan now thought of as engorged cagoules. Vanessa knew them, it seemed. She stopped, said hello, and introduced her father. Politenesses were exchanged; Alan explained that he was visiting for just under a week. "A week? Please stay longer," said the man, who seemed unduly interested in the terms of Alan's visit. Both the man and the woman had a kindly, soft-spoken manner, but also possessed the slightly condescending, sympathetic tone of the therapist, the nurse, the doctor. The dog wheezed on its leash, and jumped up. "Look after that arm, Vanessa! And God bless," said the woman, as they walked on.

They were next-door neighbors, and the last name was Dent. Jerry did something with computers. "They're evangelical Christians," said Vanessa.

"Hence the 'God bless' bit."

"They're pretty hard-core—they worship at a very *lively*, i.e., crazily charismatic church. But it's not bad, as these places go,

I have . . . Well, it's very popular, has an electronic sign outside
that says, 'The Bread of Life: Baked Fresh Every Sunday.' It's
famous."

"Oh dear. Near here?"

"In Malta."

"Malta?"

"Ha, I don't notice the names anymore! Malta is just down
the road. A nearby town."

"Like Troy."

"Exactly."

20

———

B ack inside the house, Josh was laughing, and showing
something on his laptop to Helen. He extended his arm
and brought Vanessa to his side—she still had her coat
on, and her small woolen cap—and held her next to him, so that
the three of them stood together, watching whatever it was they
were watching. Alan stayed put. He wasn't hostile to technology.
It was the dominance of the *screen* he disliked, the ubiquity of
these canny icons, the fluorescent saints staring down in lumi-
nous surveillance from every wall. The screen had replaced the
window. The abolition of privacy combined with the intensifica-
tion of privacy—everyone coddling his little relationship with
his little device. That wasn't his line—it was Vanessa's, and he
was misquoting it a bit: she had written that "technology threat-
ens the abolition of privacy and simultaneously promises the
privatization of privacy," a phrase he didn't understand at first, it
had to be explained to him; and which he then considered pure
genius, of course. (The conference was written up in *The Boston
Globe*, a piece that quoted Van's grand statement. He suddenly
realized that it must have been the conference where Vanessa and
Josh first met.)

Alan looked over at the three of them: children, really. His
first task was to bring Helen and Vanessa together after their

foolish squabble about the bowl, but he was embarrassed to do it with Josh there. The sisters seemed to have made some kind of reconciliation, anyway. "We met the neighbors," he said instead. "They go to a church in Malta." No one seemed impressed or surprised, they were still looking at the screen, so he added: "Better to worship at a Maltese church than at the *Second* Baptist Church here in town."

"Hey, you made that joke earlier," said Helen, not looking up. "Disqualified."

"And no one appreciated it sufficiently," said Alan. "So you get it again."

"The Second Baptist Church in *Houston* is, in fact, the second largest church in the United States," said Josh. "Weird, eh? It's a monster."

"How does he know this stuff?" asked Alan.

"Vanessa has been to that church in Malta," said Josh. Van looked awkward, and Alan thought that whatever Josh's intentions, exposing her like that was a bit unkind. He *must* resist the temptation to come to his elder daughter's defense. She could look after herself. He'd try to act as that Pope, the liberal one from the 1960s, put it: see everything, correct a little.

Vanessa explained, in a soft voice, that she'd been curious, as a neighbor and "as a philosopher, if that's not too pompous," about the kind of church the Dents went to, and "to see just how crazy and science-fictiony it was." The congregation was very kind, surprisingly liberal, the sermon quite intelligent, and she saw not one but two of her Skidmore students there. It's important to stay open, she added.

"You're not suddenly going to get religious, are you?" asked Helen. She imbued "religious" with several shades of disdain.

"Well, religious is just someone else's definition of what is sacred," said Vanessa. "Music is a kind of religion for you."

"I guess you're right," said Helen, minimizing the appearance of concession by paddling in her bag for her BlackBerry, pulling it out, and frowning at it. She was deciding to say something, perhaps: she closed her eyes, and stretched her long neck. She looked like a mother, thought Alan, for no reason he could quite explain.

"I might move from *my* current church, actually," said Helen. "Farewell, Sony."

"Well, this is news," said Vanessa, looking naively at Alan.

Leaving Sony, she explained, was the right thing to do at this point in her career, after several successes; she wanted to travel less. If she moved now, she was still young enough to build another career in the same industry. Corporate life didn't really suit her, she said, with an unconvincing grimace.

To Vanessa, Helen seemed as she had been since they were teenagers: intimidating, sure-footed, intimate only when under pressure. Even now, a mother, she carried with her the glamour of her erotic history, so busy and extensive, and so different from— until Josh!—Vanessa's pallid, intermittent experiments. All those rumors: Helen used to hint at intimacies with a famous producer, a guitarist, a singer. The dark-haired guy from Crash Test Dummies . . . Josh righted the imbalance, thank God. Helen had a remarkable authority of otherness that their father possessed in abundance. *Authority of otherness* was the phrase that had just formed in her head, as she watched her sister being theatrically authoritative. Like Dad, Helen had the ability to turn away from the world, from distraction and entanglements, and *become* the work she was doing, to care about it absolutely while she was performing it, to the exclusion of everything else. Alan had little fatherly authority of the traditional kind. He rarely lost his temper, wasn't irrational or physically imposing. He never bullied. His authority had to do with his ability to turn away from them and become someone else, someone who was not a father. It was the power of banishment, a royal canceling, an unblessing— kingly, in that sense, and queenly in Helen's case. In their work, they showed they could do one thing, one thing only, and master it, and she felt this singular mastery as a reproach to her own lack of worldly success. Did she lack focus, ambition, sheer strength? Had she ever had real *strength* as a philosopher? Maybe for a brief period when she was working on her Ph.D. Maybe then, for about two years, at Princeton, she cared only about philosophy, maybe in those two years she was a kind of athlete of thought, hard-edged, single-minded, possessing great physical and mental stamina. *Purity of Heart Is to Will One Thing*—she'd never read that Kierkegaard book (when you'd read one Kierkegaard you'd read them all, and *The Sickness Unto Death* was quite enough for her), but the title mocked her from the bookshelves. She didn't will one thing only. She had no purity of heart. She didn't will anything much, right now, except to continue to possess Josh. Anyway, philosophy wasn't, couldn't ever be, just *one thing*. But neither was music, or building a company. So what *was* this otherness they both had? Was it merely the ability to will a single obliterating triumph, rather than make do with several daily compromises, the very compromises that constituted life as she understood it?

Vanessa got up to go and make some coffee. She remembered spending a boring afternoon in her father's office. She was too young to understand what was going on, but was impressed by how utterly transformed Alan was, once at work—it was as if he'd put on a magic cape. He spoke a language that was almost foreign, a closed, coherent system, and he spoke it with fluent power. He expected a junior employee to entertain his nine-year-old daughter; twice, he looked up from his desk and looked *at her and right through her*: not coldly, but with efficient neglect. She imagined that Helen, so like their father in several ways, functioned similarly when at Sony.

It was Josh who drew Helen out: "Anyone who knows about the technology can see the music industry establishment is *way* behind the curve. Right? In, like, ten years there'll be no record stores, and CDs will be as outmoded as old 78s."

"It may not be quite as fast as that," said Helen, bending forward as she spoke, more animated now, the surpassed Black-Berry forgotten in her left hand, "but that's the future, yeah. Basically. A move away from the studios, also away from radio, and toward the computer, the phone, the screen."

"'Video really *did* kill the radio star,'" Josh said with excitement.

"'In my mind and in my car,'" Helen sang, with her hand over her mouth.

"It's a famous song, Dad," explained Helen. Her eyes were gleaming. "The point is, the studio isn't relevant any longer, or won't be, won't be the unit of power—not in the same way. The musicians will have greater power—"

"Because, going forward, they'll probably be recording and producing and selling themselves all at once," added Josh. "They'll own the label."

"Right. And there's justice—for decades the studios essentially shafted their musicians, imposed punitive contracts, often mismanaged the marketing. Malcolm McLaren with the Sex Pistols. And what about Motown—most of those musicians got almost nothing for their work. They had to sue Berry Gordy for royalties, yet he made a packet from the label. Do you know why you hardly ever hear crash cymbals on the classic Motown songs?"

"No, but you *will* tell me," said Josh, smiling. Quite flirtatiously, Alan thought, with sudden alarm.

"Because many of the recordings were done in what were basically the living rooms and basements of ordinary Detroit houses. The mics weren't good enough—crash cymbals would have overwhelmed them. Actually I feel pretty utopian about this. I've never been a producer, I started as basically a company accountant, because I had a degree in economics, and supposedly *knew about money*, and became 'an executive,' whatever that means. I think we're on the verge of a moment when someone like me, who was traditionally considered at best a suit and at worst the enemy, could become the ally of really great new musicians. I want to liberate them to do their best stuff. Back to a Motown sort of model, but without the exploitation. A revolution."

"That does sound utopian," said Vanessa, who had come into the room with the coffeepot. She wanted to sound as neutral as possible.

"It has to be utopian, because I'd be running a business that also functioned, at least at first, like a philanthropic foundation."

"But it couldn't be a charity, it surely has to be a business?" asked Alan.

"Oh, by the way, Dad could be involved," Helen said jubilantly.

"*Would* you?" asked Vanessa. Alan shrugged, opened his hands to the air. For a second, with both women looking at him expectantly, he was forty years old and they were young children, asking nothing more than whether he would come outside and push the swing he'd attached to the massive dusky copper beech. Mummy was bored of doing it. Nothing more: he could do that.

"Yes, I might well," he answered.

"*What* would you do?" asked Vanessa. Alan said that he wasn't sure, but that perhaps his experience in building and managing a reasonably successful company from scratch would be of help.

For some reason, a statement that would have been easy for him to utter in a familiar context made him awkward, in this house in Saratoga Springs, with another generation, perhaps two other generations, watching him. He added that he had a few business rules that had worked well for him over the years. He might get them into a book one day. Josh asked what they were, and again Alan felt strangely shy. "Well, do you know the real reason why we beat the Germans in the Second World War?"

"Wait, who's *we* . . . ? I'm just *kidding*," said Josh.

"Because we had better supply lines than the Germans did. That's a fact. The British were more efficient than the hyper-efficient Germans . . . Well, the same goes for civilian life. You're only as good as your suppliers, all the way down the chain. Sort out who supplies you, find the people you can really trust, and that's half of the work done there."

"Interesting," said Josh, turning away.

"Dad is famous for his 'rules,' in our family," said Vanessa happily. She loved being with her family. It was all she wanted, really. "Some of them make sense and others are extremely mysterious. Who wants coffee?"

"In what way mysterious?" asked Alan, mock-woundedly, smiling at Vanessa.

"Well, the one about how you should always back your car into the drive, because the journey out is more important than the return. I think that counts as practically a piece of *metaphysics* in the business world." Everyone was amused, and Alan realized that this was the first time he'd heard Josh laugh—the lad seemed to suck in air even as he expelled it.

"You also used to say," added Helen, "the one thing a parent can reliably do for his children is to give them swimming lessons, so they don't kill themselves by drowning." There was—so Alan felt—a quick silence in the room, and Helen moved on rapidly. "And you used to tease Van, when she was at her most vegetarian, that it's very hard, when eating a roast chicken, to think it wasn't expressly created to be eaten."

"Ha, I'm not sure that's a *rule*, exactly," said Alan. Vanessa, passing coffee, added a few more: Dad *always* assumed that people who had bidets in their bathrooms were into "kinky stuff." And much as he admired Nelson Mandela, it was an uncomfortable fact—Van emphasized the word "fact"—that the quality of South African white wine had declined since the end of apartheid. *And* he was oddly proud of never having had hiccups.

"You've never had the hiccups?" asked Josh.

"Not to my knowledge."

"That's a weirdly cool achievement," he said.

"You know, I think so, too," said Alan, unsure just how sarcastic Josh was being.

21

Alan sat alone in the hotel lobby. His drink was slowly rotting the paper napkin it sat on. Dixieland jazz again marched tastefully through the air. He was sunk in a fusty red velvet couch. He closed his eyes. Helen had gone to bed; it was far too late to phone Candace—he'd not spoken to her today. He felt uneasy, raw, vulnerable. At dinner—he and Helen ate together in the hotel, leaving Van and Josh for time together at home—he had revealed feelings about Josh that he had intended to keep to himself. Helen had come to the young man's defense, she was stimulated by his juvenile cockiness. Too stimulated . . . He'd seen Helen and Josh today, the way they sang that little jingle, like lovers sharing a cigarette, he'd seen that gleam in Helen's eyes. And as a father, he was put in the painful position of having to judge, from Josh's possibly aroused perspective, the relative sexiness of his daughters: yes, from that point of view, Helen was the clear winner. She had a body and she knew what to do with it. Of course, he was reacting to nothing more than a breeze of flirtation between two adults. But it made him uneasy. Not for what it revealed about Helen—she was enjoying herself, she was a social tourist, she'd be gone in two days, she was probably unaware of it—but for what it revealed about Josh and his care—that *was* the necessary word—for and of Vanessa. He was tempted to warn Helen against too obviously favoring Josh, but realized that it was essential that he say nothing at all to either daughter about the matter. Van hadn't witnessed most of the flirting—she'd gone to the kitchen to make coffee and have a smoke out back. And if he mentioned it to Helen, she might increase her attentiveness.

Josh was warm, charming, handsome. But where did the boy get that slightly tiresome confidence? At dinner, Helen said he was just young and enthusiastic. She said he was "a bit of a techno-nerd." (Though also "quite cute.") Van had said "Jewish-confrontational." Maybe that was part of it. Alan sometimes liked to indulge the fantasy that the Old Testament had been written not about the Jews, but about the British. Just imagine it for a second: the whole Bible concerns the story of . . . the British! Imagine how bloody good *we'd* feel about ourselves, imagine the deep, invisible reserves of confidence that flow from the knowledge that your little national origin story is one of the founding religious myths of the world . . . Far better, even, than having Shakespeare, Newton, and Darwin on our side. Maybe that was it. Jewish-confrontational. Or perhaps American-confrontational? He'd learned a couple of things today. Americans really did pronounce "news" as "nooze." And they apparently used the phrase "going forward," as in, "So what, going forward, should Senator Obama say about race, to neutralize the issue on the campaign trail?" (Josh pronounced the word as "*fo*ward.") Imagine the English using *that* phrase! . . . more like "going backward." One thing that united Josh and Helen, he could see it now, was their slightly utopian streak—they believed that things were changing or about to change, changing for the better. They had plans and projects. They both thought that Senator Obama had a real shot at the job. Good for them. Van seemed left out of this excitement, not just because the two were now singing silly pop songs to each other and talking about the future of music, but because all that Van truly cherished and loved, all that she studied and practiced, belonged so deeply in the past.

And what about me? Alongside Josh, he felt old and nostal-
gic and pedagogical. He didn't want to teach old lessons to new
students. Why, just before leaving Van's house, did he start on his
stupid denunciation of the computer? Josh had been saying something about how most music would soon be not just played but
composed on a computer. Irritated by his certainties, Alan said
something to the effect that maybe all this was true, but you
would never be able to go up to a computer and sing a few notes
from a melody, and ask it to identify that melody. "Not *quite*
true," said Josh, "we're getting there with solo voice recognition.
Hey, we could experiment right now with my laptop." And even
Van had a sympathetic, slightly sad look, as she jumped in: "Dad,
actually Josh has written a lot about this—there've been incredible
advances in the software." The verdict—all three agreed—seemed
to be that pretty soon you *could* go up to a computer and sing a
garbled melody and get an identification: "Beethoven Fifth, first
bar." His vulnerability nagged at him—especially that sympathetic
face of Van's. She obviously didn't want to correct her old man in
public, but history—progress, rather—forced the correction.

There was a woman sitting opposite him, on the other side
of the low glass table; he didn't know exactly how long she'd been
there. She was slightly turned away from him, perhaps to mitigate
the awkwardness. "Okay if I sit here?" she asked. "The chairs are
up on the other tables, and the bar's just closed."

"Absolutely," he answered, too quickly, in the accommodat-
ing English way. "I'm not going to stay here for long anyway."

"Oh, I've blown it again. Something I said!" She grinned,
and he understood that she'd had a few drinks, and that maybe
she often had a few drinks. He reckoned her to be five or so years
younger than him. Her dyed black hair was past due—a frozen
white stream, the late fee as it were, ran right down the middle
of her parting. She looked a little wrecked, had the undernour-
ished plumpness of the drinker. But everyone more or less his age
looked wrecked; you became slightly fond of *everyone* your age,

as maybe you were once fond of everyone in your football team or in your regiment. If he saw wreck, what on earth did she see in him?

"Where are you from?" she asked.

"England. I'm visiting my daughter here."

"Yeah, I thought so—you have a great accent. Like one of the Beatles."

"Oh no, that's Liverpool, further south . . . thanks anyway."

"I've been to England," she said. "To London. Also Cornwall. It rained . . . *like shit* the whole time. You don't mind me saying that?"

"It does. Rain a lot. Like shit, in fact. Was that recently?" He guessed that it wasn't, that recent life involved drinking and sleeping it off, and hanging around this town. He found her quite attractive, partly because she was opposite him and talking to him, but not only because of that—there was some grandeur in her manners, a ruined prestige that intrigued him. He liked her American drawl, her deep voice, and her eyes, which looked sore.

"I went there as a kid, a few times. Twice on a boat, once in a plane. No, twice in a plane . . . Oh hell, whatever. Twice in a boat, and twice on a plane, I think . . . We're not allowed to smoke here, right? Do you think anyone would stop us? That little fascist at the bar would—he just invented a *bullshit state law* that says he's not allowed to serve someone more than three drinks in one hour." Her voice was rising and Alan was keen to go to bed and leave her to the persuasive force of the little fascist, but he didn't want to seem rude, so he asked her why she'd gone so often to England when she was small. She told him that she grew up in New York City, with money and privilege—a nanny, a cook, a Hungarian driver. A big apartment on Park Avenue. And an English father. My mother, she said, was a Trask. It sounded like some kind of religious sect, or perhaps a political sinecure. A Trask? She explained that Trask was a surname, and that her mother's nineteenth-century forebears bought a large estate just outside Saratoga Springs. In the 1890s, they built a huge house on their land, designed it to look like a famous country house in England—she forgot which one. "It's called Yaddo. Have you heard of it?" He had not, but then he'd only been in town for two days. The name, she said, came from one of the Trask children, who invented it, to rhyme with "shadow." The daughter loved the way the maple trees cast shadows. The Trasks bequeathed their house, in the 1920s, to America's creative artists, stipulated that Yaddo had to be used as a writers' retreat, a place for people to come and do creative work. It wasn't open to the public, so he'd never be able to visit it. "Unless your daughter's a writer."

How, he asked, did the Trask heirs feel about their ancestral home being given over in perpetuity to a bunch of freeloading artists?

"Honey," she said, pausing theatrically to drain her empty wineglass, "that's the point. There were no direct heirs, it's the saddest fucking story—the Trasks lost all four of their children in childhood. All four. Diphtheria, mostly." Alan agreed that it was terribly sad—the great horror, he thought to himself, the reversal of generation, parents burying their children, Karl Marx trying to throw himself into the grave to lie alongside his young son.

"I know something about that," she said. "About sad fucking stories." She looked at him, and ordinary decency demanded that he ask her more. But he was tired, and couldn't quite face the spillage of another ten minutes. And didn't he have his own sad stories? So he looked down at his drink, and she fortunately lost the black thread of her sad tale, and also went quiet. Grabbing his moment, he made his apologies, told her he'd enjoyed their conversation, and stood up.

"*You're* not the only who has to go," she said with quick annoyance. "Didn't I say, two minutes ago, I couldn't stay for long?"

"Okay," he said, gently surrendering to her fiction. "Okay."

•

Back in his room, he stood by the freezing window. Outside it was clear, dry, arctic—the over-salted main street was parched gray like desert bone, the packed walls of snow glowing blue in the streetlamps. He watched her leave the hotel, stop to light a cigarette, fumble the fag and pick it up, and then walk slowly, far too slowly for the frigid temperature, up Broadway.

On his way to the bathroom, he passed the closed white laptop on his desk. It had made its way out of the computer bag, but no further. Yes, he should log on and see if Eric Ball had written to him. Two other colleagues, also. Worst of all—the three-year migraine of the Dobson Arts Centre and Café; movement on that project was promised this week or next. He would not open the magic box and let all the evils fly around the room. It could wait till morning.

22

He woke to snow, continuous snowing. Broadway was utterly empty, the parched asphalt of last night resurfaced in fresh white. It was coming down fast, in the passive-aggressive way of snow, stealthy but relentless, insisting on its own white agenda, the soft monotony canceling all time, all resistance, all activity. Alan surrendered to the silent vacancy, the pure negative that was like some terrible ideal death. The Trask children, good God. His father died on a snowy day like this. Da went almost blind in his last week, so Alan had to put his face very close to his father's as he lay in the hospital bed. "What do you see now, Da?" he asked, and his weary father replied, in a clotted voice, "I see a *kind face*." They were his last coherent words, and more intense, more emotional certainly, than anything he had said when in his right mind and body . . . But Josh's laugh— *not* kind, not kind at least to Alan. Leave it, leave it. There were important things to do, nothing would be achieved by fretting over the question of Josh and Vanessa. He had to be of practical help, to be of *use* in whatever way he could offer. And the best step was to get his own house in order—talk first of all to Candace, then open the damned laptop, communicate with Eric about the Dobson project, do some bill paying . . .

Bill paying: it had been a mistake to open an office in Manchester. There was nothing going on in Manchester, or nothing that he could afford. He'd arrived too late, was standing on a finished plateau. Like Alex Ferguson signing Rio Ferdinand for all that money—an absolute disaster really, pound for pound—only to discover that Ferdinand's best football was largely behind him. The Manchester office was expensive, and diverted two employees from Newcastle just to man the place, where they sat twiddling their thumbs and attending to their e-mails and their late-night clubbing plans. The recent website design had been bizarrely pricey. Alan had assumed that near-invisible work would come with a near-invisible price tag, and tried not to reveal his astonishment when Eric told him what they finally owed the Mormon and his Salt Lake City design company.

More grievous than this small stuff was the collapse of property values in the four northern cities where Querry Holdings owned their biggest buildings. They badly needed to sell the Seddon, in Sunderland, a mixed residential-commercial building that had only ever been half-occupied anyway. They needed to do that in order to pay other bills, including the interest on the big Lloyds loan, taken out in order to grease the wheels of the Dobson project in Newcastle—a push-me-pull-you situation that Alan had sworn he would never get into. But nobody was interested in the Seddon, even when they dropped the price at the end of last year by a sick-making thirty percent. Dynamic pricing, ha . . . And it was the same with two properties for sale in York, a city that for years had been a solidly reliable market. The company was small—ten employees, counting him—and it never had enormous liquidity. It had thrived by going for shrewd opportunities and by keeping costs fairly low. The company *was* him, and was *like* him: an efficient frame, a lean strength, and a sensible ratio of energy in and energy out.

He had grown up in a time and place of corrupt city councilmen, illegalities and criminalities, viciously amoral landlords, with the threat of violence hanging over everything like a parental prohibition. *Get Carter* was a tame fantasy—the milky-skinned

Michael Caine with his Cockney accent wouldn't have lasted a day in the real Newcastle. He was branded on his tongue: an outsider. That Newcastle pub—Alan knew it well—at the start of the film: Caine would have had to wait a lot longer than five insultingly slow minutes to get a tall glass of beer. How about never? How's never for you? Alan had no interest in that world, had no interest in doing business if it also meant doing harm, so he ignored it, doubtless another reason he was not in the top tier, probably not even the second or third tier, of property developers in the North East. Well, so be it: he was proud that his company had served only two eviction notices in thirty years. Two. He had *had* plenty of appetite, will, hunger to succeed . . . but not at any cost. *I see a kind face.* Could you be a kind, successful business-man? Too often these days, he could hear his late dad saying to him, "Look at any man who has amassed a great fortune, and you're looking at a bloody crook." He thought Da was right, basically, which perhaps explained why, at sixty-eight, he was neither a crook (or so he thought) nor (alas) the keeper of a great fortune. Still, it was one thing not to want great riches, and an-other to be squandering what reasonably comfortable reserves had been built up over the years. One thing not to be a ruthlessly successful capitalist, and another to be a *failed* capitalist, bleeding money from self-inflicted wounds. He'd done this *to himself*—that's what caused pain. He had been seduced—no, he'd seduced *himself* with the idea of expansion: more employees, another office, more buildings, partly because everyone else was expanding, too, and you felt like a comparative failure if you didn't secure your feeding place along with everyone else at the piggery.

Rather than open the box of tricks, he'd phone Eric Ball. It would be just after lunchtime on Sunday, back in Newcastle. Eric would be doing one of two things: biking (he was a fanatical cyclist, had all the gear: the bantamweight Chinese-made bike, the scarab-beetle helmet, the orange-and-yellow spandex mem-brane, whose trousers made a drama out of Eric's punished genitals and always put Alan in mind of male ballet dancers and their mysterious, packeted groins) or watching sports on telly or preparing to watch sports on telly. Eric happily watched any televised sport, however dull it was, like a scholar content amid the most tedious footnotes.

He got Eric's machine, and couldn't help smiling as he heard the familiar Yorkshire accent, flat, nasal, pedantic—"You've *nearly* reached Eric Ball"—and began to leave a message when Eric picked up.

"I didn't recognize the number. How are you?"

"So I've *actually* reached Eric Ball." A tediously old joke.

"Right! . . . We were meant to be out on a ten-mile hill climb, but the weather . . . You didn't get my e-mail, or even the message, then?"

"It's snowing in Saratoga Springs. Snowing! I haven't opened my laptop. No time. It's all work here—different from real work, but still work, you know."

"Yikes, you want the bad news first, or the really bad news?"

"Oh Christ."

"The city's pulling the plug on the Dobson project. They're withdrawing all the subsidies. So it's basically dead as far as I can see."

"Why, for God's sake?"

"Because the carpenters' union has announced that they're suing the city for the right to the contracts."

"The carpenters? UCATT? Our problem was supposedly going to be with the cement guys."

"It's never the one you bloody expect, is it? Watch out for the nig . . . the weevil . . . in the woodpile. Worm in apple, whatever. Anyway, the carpenters are arguing that because of the way the project is structured it's a government project, not a private deal, so that they have legal rights to a share of the job."

"Which would basically double our costs," said Alan, aware

now that the hotel telephone receiver wasn't very clean—the mouthpiece seemed a bit gluey.

"Right. Well, *that*, added to the atrocious cost projection that SGR did last week, seems to have turned the city bigwigs off the whole bloody thing."

"But we've invested an effing *boatload*. And we got permission to knock down a whole warehouse for this!"

"We got the notification on Friday, and I've been trying to get hold of you. I'm worried, Alan."

Friday was when he was on the train with Helen, talking about getting "involved" in her new company.

"The partners agree with this? David and Lee? They're dropping it, too?"

"It's because *they're* dropping it that we have to. They told *me*. We can't do this on our own, we just don't have the cash."

"Eric, we need to shift the bloody Seddon. I don't care what it takes, we get that building off the books. The interest payments on the Lloyds loan, those alone, are *crippling* us."

"Well, we've had no luck yet, have we? But I'll get to it first thing tomorrow. I'm on it, okay? We'll shift the Seddon."

"This is bloody, bloody bad news."

•

Some projects were cursed, like haunted houses or crap cars. And the ones that were cursed were always those whose completion you could most vividly imagine. The building rose up before him, finished, gleaming, functional—all that was needed was Harrison Ford and a hundred Amish men in breeches and the thing could be up in a day . . . The Dobson project was like that. He *knew* it could work, he knew how good it would look, but no one else agreed with him. That's why he had invested so much in it.

When he stopped to think about it, a kind of vertigo or

nausea made him sit down heavily on the side of the bed. So it was important not to think about it. Leave it, leave it.

Strangely, a minute or two later, he felt almost liberated. He remained on the bed. "Trying to get hold of you," Eric had said. It was almost *exciting* to be off the grid. He would lose a fair bit of money, a lot of money, but it was *just money*, what Cathy, mimicking her headmaster father, used to call "filthy lucre"—in her poshest, non-northern accent. What if he didn't talk again to Eric while he was over here in the States? Didn't open the computer at all this week? What if he just turned away from it, turned away from the whole thing, toward something else? Helen's new project, for instance—he could dedicate the, what, last ten or fifteen years of his life to *that*. He wasn't handing on the Querry company to anyone, it wasn't a family business—neither daughter was interested. Right enough, there: they had their own lives. But when he thought about handing the company on, or not handing it on, he felt that vertiginous nausea again . . . death; the Hadrian's Wall experience . . . No. He wouldn't think about *that*. He'd known, from early on, the company probably wouldn't survive his death. But he was traditional enough to want to leave money and property for those who survived him. He must provide for Helen and Vanessa, now for Candace, too, and what was horrifying to him was the thought of letting them down, of leaving little or nothing—or worse, debts and mountainous complexities.

These days, he was always hearing about "reducing one's footprint"—Vanessa had said it about Josh, and everyone in the news now talked about "minimizing the carbon footprint." He disliked the phrase. Like any sane person, he didn't want to reduce his footprint, he wanted to increase it. His last name wouldn't survive, but at least there might be an old family house for them all to return to, and some cash in the bank for everyone. The terror that it might all collapse, that he might die unexpectedly, prematurely, before he'd sorted things out, before his *own mother* had died . . . that weighed heavily. One of his most precious possessions was the Festival of Britain brochure he brought back in 1951, from London. It sat in a drawer of his desk at home. Full of proud advertisements for old British companies that either no longer existed or had been bought up by larger foreign corporations, or broken apart by huge, mysterious private equity groups— Crompton Bulbs and Manfield Shoes and HMV Records. Dunlop Rubber. Pilkington Glass. (The windows of his Audi were made by Pilkington, which pleased him. But the company was now owned by the Japanese.) The cars: Triumph, Morris, MG, Riley, Rover, Jaguar. The advert for Bass and Worthington Ale announced, in words his whole class at school patriotically memorized, years before they could drink a pint of Bass: *He who plants an avenue of trees cannot, in the nature of things, hope to enjoy them in their grandeur—he plants them for England . . . We, too, must keep this tradition of the thing well made, that our children's children may be beholden to us.*

He would never forget the moment when his father asked to borrow a hundred pounds from him. Alan was twenty-seven, and had just made his first bit of serious money. He felt the reversal of authority like a roaring original sin: wrong, wrong! Of course he lent his father the money, and would have lent him, surreptitiously, ten times as much, if he'd had it. But he was embarrassed that his father was embarrassed; he hated to see him *ask*.

23

An hour later, he had breakfast with Helen. It was still snowing; the hotel had the slightly excited, pumped-up atmosphere of unthreatening crisis: emergency relief for the pampered. Staff tramped in and out of the lobby, large boots squeaking on the wood floor. White lengths of snow, like fluorescent stripes, were caught in the folds of their nylon coats. The lights seemed to dim and flicker every so often; Alan thought he might be imagining it. Not so, said Helen. American infrastructure was "crap, relatively speaking." It's become, she said, a country of patching—everywhere you look there are crews patching roads, patching bridges, patching sewers, roofs, telephone wires. "Maybe that'll change if a Democrat is elected president next year. Or maybe it won't."

Helen was strangely bright. With calm, controlling movements, she played mum. She poured Alan's coffee from the heavy hotel pot, and then milk from the tiny stainless steel Hunca Munca jug. She asked the waiter to bring Alan orange juice. As usual, she sat very upright. She smiled freshly at him. Even by Helen's standards, it was an unusual display of vigor.

"I have an idea, I've been thinking," she said. He bent his head. The coffee in his pleasing white mug smelled of morning and bitter resolve. And discretion and keeping your bloody trap shut. "I've been thinking about how we should all get together

this summer—maybe *not* in Northumberland, maybe somewhere in France or Italy? Have a family reunion that really in-
cludes Tom and the twins, and Josh and Van? There's that lovely
hotel on the Sorrento coast, lemon trees everywhere, the one
Tom and I went to for our honeymoon? We could all spend some
time together. Candace and Van would actually get to know the
twins, and Josh would meet everyone and feel part of the family."

"Not cheap," said Alan, witnessing his inescapable parsimony
with dislike.

"Well, reason not the need. No—reason not the *deed*, I
guess," said Helen, with brisk condescension. "If we start counting the pennies, we won't do anything ever, I certainly wouldn't
be thinking about leaving Sony, for instance."

"Ah, we should talk about that," said Alan, preemptively,
because he didn't want to talk about it now.

"If a hotel doesn't work, we can always do it in Northumberland, but we might be more festive somewhere that didn't remind
us so much of Mum."

"No, no, it's a good idea. We've actually never done anything
like that as a whole family, since Cathy, since Mum . . . Assum-
ing we'd all get on with each other."

"Obviously, Van and Josh wouldn't be able to afford it, so you
and I would pick up their costs," Helen said with certainty. She'd
always been like this. She would run down the stairs from her
bedroom and announce, eyes shining, that she had dreamed up a
mail-order business so that she could resell her old shoes. Or: She
and Vanessa would go house to house, mowing people's lawns.
She and Van would teach guitar (Helen) and piano (Van) to
beginners. Cathy had rather decided, middle-class views about the
impropriety of hawking oneself around the village for sale, but
Alan was amused and supportive, partly because he knew each
enterprise would collapse like the last.

"We'd all get on because we'd make an effort to get on.
Maybe Van and Josh should spend the whole of this summer in

England and get a feel for the place. Van's been away so long it's
a different country now, and Josh has never been. And why
couldn't Van start looking for a job in the U.K.? I mean, she's
not *condemned* to spend the rest of her life in Saratoga Springs, is
she? Why shouldn't she teach philosophy back in Britain?"

"Well, I can think of one reason," said Alan.

"Yes, Josh. But Van needs to think of herself first, and it's
mad that she should rusticate, *vegetate*, in upstate New York for
Josh. See, I care so much about it I'm rhyming! If they're devot-
ing whole conferences to her work, then maybe she could teach
at—I don't know!—Oxford or Cambridge or London? She's
certainly good enough. Isn't she?"

Helen was leaning forward on her chair, her broad, slightly
thickened shoulders filling the space before him, as vigorous and
palpable as her plans. A posture he knew, twice over—Cathy
used to lean forward like this. Sometimes the similarities were
like a shocking plagiarism, an outrageous laziness on the part of
the family genes.

"And Josh?"

"Oh, Dad, I'm not sure—"

"Not sure about what?" he said. He carefully placed his coffee cup on the table.

"He has guilty eyes."

"Come on, Helen. That's not really good enough, is it?"

"I don't know if . . . I wonder if Josh really intends to *stick
around*, if you want my very honest opinion."

Alan now realized that Helen's restless planning, her fizzing
impatience, her ideas about family holidays and magical, unlikely
jobs at Oxford and Cambridge probably flowed from a new anxiety about her sister's future. She could see something that he could
not. Perhaps it was obvious to her *precisely* because Josh had been
flirting with her? Helen *saw* things like that, much more clearly
and decisively than he did.

"I *would* like to know," said Alan, looking earnestly at his daughter.

"It's just a feeling I got yesterday. And also something Josh said to me seemed ominous."

"What did he say?"

"No, no, don't panic, it was a small thing, so don't make too much of it. Maybe I'm reading too much into it. He talked about wanting to live and work in New York."

"Well, what's the problem?"

"New York City, Dad, not New York State. Because he only talked about himself. He said 'I,' not 'we.' When *I* get to New York."

"That is a small thing," said Alan, with manufactured relief.

"Maybe. But I had two boyfriends—Stephen and Roly, remember them?—whose announced plans always seemed to omit me, and you know where *those* relationships went."

"You have so much more experience in these things than Van!"

"Well," she replied, returning to her earlier briskness, "I do things, and Van thinks things. Though *I* think, too, you know."

"I know you do."

•

They were the last people at breakfast, their table the last spoiled one amid the prepared perfection. The barman had arrived, was already tuning up his instruments for lunch. The snow was lighter, the flakes had almost ceased: a few frail laggards fluttered down. Alan pushed his chair out, preparing to leave.

"Dad, before you go: this stuff about leaving Sony . . . You said yesterday that you might get involved in my new project. Did you mean it, or were you being nice?"

"Couldn't it be both?"

"You know I'm not bullshitting, right? There's a revolution

happening. That book I showed you on the train . . . The authors say that very soon music will be like water, flowing freely through pipes and networks and plumbing, straight into people's homes. It'll be a fact of life. Like turning on a tap. You'll pay a flat fee for the right to turn on the tap. And that'll be that. The record companies, though, still want you to buy water in little expensive bottles—Perrier, Evian. Imagine trying to fill your bath with little bottles of Evian! That's how the big record companies are still thinking. But it's not the future. The future is the tap, not the little bottle of Evian. That's what the book is arguing."

"This makes sense, I suppose. Though music isn't as essential as water, of course. The plumbing is supposed to be—what? The Internet?" The more enthusiastic she got, the calmer he would be.

"Yes, essentially—digital communication of all kinds, streaming and sharing services. You saw yesterday when Josh got so excited?"

Alan thought: when you both got so excited.

"That's because," Helen continued, "he knows about this stuff, it's his world. He can see a big change coming. They all can. And I want to be there. Do you know what David Bowie said, in 2002—in 2002! He wrote an article about how the absolute transformation of everything that anyone has ever thought about music is imminent, and nothing is going to stop it. He predicted *then* that copyright would no longer exist in ten years."

"That last fact sounds like a headache, actually, from your point of view."

"It doesn't matter whether it sounds like a headache or an orgasm, it's what's going to happen!"

They both knew that she hadn't quite intended to say "orgasm." Alan looked down at his hands.

"And yes, I do think it's exciting," she added.

"Clearly." They smiled.

"So it's an opportunity. You should understand that. You

always used to say that you were good at looking for opportunities."

"Did I?"

"All the time. Well, that's what it will take—the ability to look for opportunities. We'll need not to overextend ourselves in the first few years, because profits may be limited to begin with."

"We?"

"But as long as we're patient and can see ahead, and keep on reminding ourselves that *the record business is not the music business*, then I think we could build something that is really exciting, which could become a whole factory for a brilliant new generation of British musicians." Her eyes were dazzling, her chin was thrust up—she was the twelve-year-old girl on Christmas Day, holding her new three-quarter-sized Yamaha acoustic guitar, the crushed wrapping paper blooming on the carpet, announcing with passionate confidence: "I'll play this properly by the summer!"

"*We*," Helen continued impatiently, "would be you and me and anyone else we can get to commit to the project. I'll need at least three or four major investors. I have some shares I can liquidate, but that won't be nearly enough. Tom is being cautious and wary, of course, so he's basically an obstacle I'll have to work around."

"I promise not to be an obstacle you have to work around. That doesn't sound like a good fate at all."

"The thing is, Dad," she began. "Look, do you want a bit more coffee? Why don't I get a fresh pot?" She raised an imperious hand for the waiter. "Here's the thing. I know I said, on the train, that I don't need any financial help. That's quite true."

"But not quite true?" he said.

"Not quite true," she conceded. Her arm was still raised.

"In what way?"

"In the way that a half-truth is also a half-lie, depending on whether you see the glass as half-full or half-empty."

"I see. Well, I guess I do."

"Of course I need money," said Helen, "but I would only *think* of asking you if you told me that you want to be involved. If not, not—you're totally free to walk away. No big deal. And of course, it wouldn't be *help*, but a loan, an investment, a business proposition."

"Helen, dear—my love! This is a lot to consider. Let me think about this. Just let me *think*." He repeated himself more aggressively than he meant to.

"I'm sorry that I asked."

"No no, please stop that."

"Stop apologizing, or stop asking?" Helen was grim, flushed, solid, in a way he recognized.

"I would like to help. This is an opportunity. But just at the moment—"

"Well, I'm not asking you to get the checkbook out right now at the table, for God's sake."

"It's that . . . just now," he continued, feeling as if he were trying to make his way up the main street outside, walking straight into driving snow, "things are somewhat up in the air at the company. The Dobson project, you heard me talking about it *years* ago probably, has just fallen through, so a big loan has to be repaid. Profits are down. We have very little of a buffer. And cash flow is not readily available at the moment."

Helen would remember that last phrase, "cash flow is not readily available at the moment."

"But surely, it's in the nature of what you do"—and yet, she realized, she had so little idea of what he really did—"that things succeed and fail, and rise and fall. No? You *can't* be telling me that you or the company has no money. That's just *ridiculous*. That's not true."

"It's no business of yours how much or how little money I have," he said quickly.

"Fine, and it's no business of yours what I do with the next twenty years of my life. You won't hear me talk about it ever again."

"I'm sorry, Helen, I don't want to hurt you. But please listen to me—we're comfortable rather than rich. *You* know that. So we need to proceed cautiously. Just give me a little more time." He sounded like a debtor, and she the creditor. So he rephrased himself, more calmly. "I promise you that we will have this conversation again, in a few weeks, without anger, but certainly not *in public*, all right?"

"No we won't." She rose from the table.

"Come on, Helen."

"It's okay, Dad," she said more gently, and grandly, theatrically even, "*I absolve you.*" She touched his head as she passed behind him, and walked out of the dining room.

24

Her father had never understood her music—and so he had never really understood her. That was her conclusion as she went up to her room. Dad didn't understand, Van had never properly understood. Tom didn't, really. Who, then? Julian Vereker, her first boyfriend, lovely Jules, the refusenik drummer of Jensen and the Interceptors—who had actually quit their band, comically enough, because, he said, "I'm sick of being the one who is always in charge of ending the songs!" He was a lousy drummer, but he loved music in the same way as she did. They used to lie on the floor, holding hands, between his parents' ridiculously large Wharfedale hi-fi speakers. Julian reeked of his teenager's vulgar aftershave . . . Denim, it was called.

Music was now her official life; and much more important, it was her secret joy. Because *she* was really the girl—not Jenny—in "Rock & Roll," who felt that *nothing was happening at all*, until *one fine morning* she turned on a New York radio station and *couldn't believe what she heard*. When she was twelve, Helen turned on the radio, and heard—not Lou Reed, but Joe Jackson's "It's Different for Girls," and that was that. Not Jenny's New York radio; not "Mohammed's Radio" either (sweet song, that one); but *her* radio, which played always inside her.

Music had been far more reliable than friends or parents or lovers. It never abandoned her, it was always there to teach and

instruct, console and excite. Songs structured her life. What philosophy was to Van, music was to Helen. She didn't just *like* the
songs—that was what ordinary people felt—but took them inside her. Joe Jackson spoke to her because she was just beginning
to feel, at almost thirteen, that it was definitely different for girls.
Four years later, she *was* actually the girl who left the north for
Euston station, *with this really ragged notion that you'll return*, as
that great Smiths song went. (She never really did return. It was
King's Cross, but close enough.) She once told a cruel boyfriend
to *try a little tenderness*, because Otis Redding said he should.
(For years, she had thought Otis's *same old shaggy dress* was a
shabby one.) At her school, the boy hero, the sporty handsome
boy all the girls fell in love with—*he is of pure and noble breed*—
was *actually* called, no kidding, David Watts, just as the Jam said
he was! Her first kiss happened at a party (joss sticks and crimson lightbulbs) while the Human League was clicking out "Don't
You Want Me"—tinny music from tinny speakers, but a real
kiss. (She did want, she did.) Long before she experienced an
orgasm, she had an idea—no: more than an idea, a feeling right
between her legs—of what that event might be like, from the
cosmic climax, the stellar *come*, that the scandalously underpaid
Clare Torry screamed out in "The Great Gig in the Sky." When
she went through a phase of political rebellion, "The Eton Rifles"
and "Cortez the Killer" and "Won't Get Fooled Again" gave her
the words, lent her the energy and excitement: *Meet the new boss,
same as the old boss.* (And the Sex Pistols, with their stunning
aggression and their funny, trilling, Dalek voices.) Radiohead's
"No Surprises" and Ian Dury's "You'll See Glimpses"—the best
and saddest song of all—always made her think of Van, and of
Van's precarious happiness. (Van, Van!) And when her mother
was dying, Helen wept and wept at Peter Gabriel's beautiful
"Wallflower," and its hopeful coda: *And I will do what I can do.*
(She could do nothing, of course.)

    And for joy and dancing? Martha and the Muffins, "Echo

Beach." Dancing to that song at university, at four in the morning, at that party after the end-of-term gig, when her own fairly crappy Oxford band (Ironic Erection) had played onstage alongside the best-known Cambridge band (President Reagan Is Not Clever). Or even better: the first time she ever heard Tammi Terrell and Marvin Gaye sing "Ain't Nothin' Like the Real Thing."

Well, there ain't nothin' like the real thing, and the real thing was rock music, and she had experienced it.

Had Dad ever understood that? Any of it? He once said he liked "You'll See Glimpses." A big concession. And he certainly implied, more than once, that he fancied "the dark-haired one in Abba." Ah! Okay.

Why secret? Why a *secret* joy? Because rock and roll, as she understood it, wants to destroy the stupid comfort of the world: *Search and destroy.* That was the atrocious and rather unfunny irony of being a record company suit . . . Rock music, the rock and roll she liked, wanted to tear down the Sony tower. (Obviously, she could *never* confess this to anyone, but this faith of hers explained her increasing boredom around the Dave Matthews Band. *Where's the garlic?* Frank Zappa's all-important question. Universally applicable, she felt.) The world had always told Helen to "put away childish things." Her fancy schools had groomed her for work, for the taming of eros, prepared her to dress in the right uniform, make obeisance to pragmatism, success, and financial self-aggrandizement. Everything existed to be made *use of.* "Life" was conceived of as entirely pragmatic—work, office nonsense, commuting, relentless haste and fatigue, imperfect weekends, a bit of sleep: that was "the world." And that was where she had ended up: economics, the "wise" choice at university; days spent inside an office. Life was something else, too. It was endless loss: Mum. Growing up had turned out to be something like the Roman *ave atque vale*, simultaneously an opening and closing, a welcome that was really a long farewell. There was no help, no protection from suffering. Two things slowed down this steady movement, this laborious death march, two young facts argued against it: children and rock and roll. And really, they were the same thing. "Put away childish things," said the world, and "come and join the reasonable grown-ups." But rock opened up that barely tolerated space for childishness, for refusal and resistance, for anti-enlightenment, for juvenile irresponsibility and revolt and blissed-out trance. Childishness, really.

For you look at your children and think: This is what we once were; and what we should be again.

The greatest musicians were children, stayed childlike, irresponsible, curiously innocent. They died young, sacrificed themselves, messed up their health and their bodies, so that we can go on living our lives, the long reasonable bourgeois sleep that is our life, tediously tending our bank accounts and dividends, our retirement funds and dinner parties and haircuts and regular dental visits. Rock music is opposed to this. It is the *sleep of reason.*

25

Vanessa was surprised to see her father—he was almost an hour early for lunch. She asked him where Helen was.

"I don't know if she'll join us. She's being very unreasonable."

"Uh-oh—is it my fault? Come in. It's freezing out there."

Alan gave his version of the argument. Helen's impatience, of course, was characteristically overwhelming—the whole family knew what *that* was like—and, well, when Alan suggested he'd need time to think about the money, "Helen just blew up. Just blew up."

Vanessa, unexpectedly, took Helen's side. "Dad, you did say yesterday that you might help her"—and seeing his face tighten, because Vanessa knew exactly what Alan was hiding, had intuited what the argument had really been about, she corrected herself, and added, "you did say that you might be able to be involved in some way . . ."

"Help, help," Alan muttered insultingly as he removed his coat and icy shoes.

"Helen does have such a big temper. She wants so *much*, and her disappointment is always proportionate, right?" She looked sympathetically, hopefully, at him, as she had always done, always trying to make peace, even in those periods when she was really the cause of the strife. "Would you like a cup of tea," she asked almost shyly as they walked into the kitchen. "A cuppa?"

"I'd love one . . . Good lord," he added as he sat at the pine table and looked outside, "I don't know how you manage the winters in this place." What had been a scattered white freshness in the early morning, when it was still snowing, was now a solid white tedium. It was eleven in the morning, but it might have been four in the afternoon.

"Before I came to live here, I only understood conceptually the phrase you used to hear about old or sick people—he or she *won't survive another winter.* That's what it's like here: each winter is some kind of test of survival. And your body seems to know when spring arrives, that it's gained another lease on life. It's successfully finished another precarious chapter. You can actually *feel* yourself unclenching."

Alan was worried by this talk of death and precarious survival, though Van hadn't spoken gloomily.

"I think I met one of your local 'figures' last night. A woman in the hotel bar, very keen to tell me she was a Trask, which didn't mean anything, I'm afraid. Hello there," he said as Josh appeared in the doorframe. He realized he had failed to use the lad's first name.

"Yep, we know her well," said Vanessa. "She's a figure around town, isn't she, babe?"

"She has a hip flask to get her through the dry hours. Hi, Alan, by the way!" Josh was fiddling with the coffee machine, and Alan wondered if he had just woken. Hard to tell, when your day clothes and night clothes have become essentially indistinguishable—one continuous grayish habit. Today Josh was wearing dark tracksuit bottoms, and another gray T-shirt, this one with bloodred lettering: GEORGE BUSH AND SON. FAMILY BUTCHERS. EST. 1989. In spite of himself—in spite of Josh— Alan liked the shirt.

"Poor thing, there's not much evidence she's a Trask. It seems to be her fantasy. It allows her to tell everyone her own sad tale," said Vanessa. Alan felt sorry for the woman he thought of as "the Trask lady."

"I like the shirt," he said.

"Thanks. It's a very demure piece, I think! I can't wait till the end of this dynasty. *Asses* of evil . . . I'm glad your guy is going soon, too."

"My guy?"

"Blair—rotten to the core," said Josh. "That's harsh, maybe. But tarnished—tarnished all the way down to his once-silver tongue."

Alan thought: still better than *your guy*—murderous, imbecilic, ill-educated, swaggering cowboy.

"He's not as bad as Bush, of course," said Josh, eerily divining Alan's thoughts. "On the other hand, Blair's sin is greater because his intelligence is greater. All he had to do was refuse to be part of it, like Chirac. *Je réfuse!* And unlike Chirac, he'd have gone down as a great prime minister, even if it wasn't quite true."

"I completely agree," said Alan. It was oddly tiring, conversing with Josh. The boy didn't really converse: he *waited*. Conversation as ambush.

"Unfortunately, I don't have much faith that things are going to get better," said Alan, asserting himself. "Blair's successor will offer more of the same, and then Labour will probably lose the next election, thanks to Blair and Iraq, and it'll be even worse when the Conservatives get in."

"We don't have a Barack Obama on the horizon in Britain," said Vanessa. Alan liked that "we."

"I only know what I read in the papers. I hope he'll win. But could Senator Obama do everything he promises? Do you both really believe in Obama?" asked Alan. "I wonder if he would be able to maintain the authority he would need, being black and all."

"Dad! This is America, not the north of England," said Vanessa, smiling a bit uncertainly. "Block your ears, Josh."

"That's the 'is America *ready* for a black president?' argument," said Josh briskly. "To which the answer is: no, we aren't ready. Not at all. Which is exactly why we need a black president. I think he could change the country."

"I'm not making an 'argument,' I'm just reflecting—you know—what you hear people say," complained Alan, trying to hide his wounded irritation.

"Or why we need a female president," said Vanessa. "We have to convert the present-at-hand into the ready-to-hand. Obama is currently unready-to-hand. I *think*."

"What the hell? You're mad," said Josh, smiling.

"Heidegger. I'm reading him with the German philosophy reading group. Remember—tonight? I'm plugging away at him, but I don't think I'm quite 'getting' him. A very difficult philosopher, Dad. Famous for his impenetrability. I can give you the original German terms, if you want."

"*Nein, nein!* Keep the old Nazi out of this house," Josh said, pulling Vanessa's head to his chest and kissing the top of her head.

"Actually, Dad, I invited a few of the members round tonight, to meet you and Helen. They won't stay very long. They're very interested in you."

Alan tried to look positive. On the train, Helen had said that she could endure her time in Saratoga Springs only if Vanessa didn't inflict on them "dull and pretentious academics dressed like Mr. Bean." Alan had a feeling they might be dressed like Josh rather than Mr. Bean. Perhaps they would arrive with customized T-shirts, each bearing a loud philosophical motto. Which wouldn't mean they weren't also dull and pretentious. It was typical of Vanessa—so unworldly, really—to ignore all the possible ways in which he and Helen might not want to spend time with her university colleagues. He had a feeling it was going to be a long day.

26

The German philosophy reading group looked quite normal, in the end. There were three of them; two arrived together at the house, just after six that evening. Alan was relieved to learn they were coming only for drinks. Amy Isaacson and Gary Mulhall were colleagues of Van's at Skidmore, in philosophy and English, respectively. They were around Vanessa's age, give or take a year or two; both American, one originally from Maryland and the other from the Midwest—pleasant, open, dressed in jeans and sweaters. Alan liked them both, enough that, loosened a little by his first drink, he had to catch himself from sharing certain family intimacies. He'd been on the verge of asking them what they knew about Vanessa's broken arm, and how she had seemed to them these last few months. The third guest arrived fifteen minutes later, and didn't seem to fit. He was much older than the other two; Alan put him in his late seventies. He made Vanessa anxious: she opened the door, exclaimed, and immediately called for Josh to come and help; she prematurely offered her guest champagne while he was struggling to hang up his large, old-fashioned woolen overcoat. He was formally dressed—jacket, crimson handkerchief in the breast pocket—and his manners were reticent. Around the edges of his American accent were the traces, perhaps, of a lost European life—he lingered on his *t*'s, and sprinkled umlauts over the needier vowels. He'd obviously been handsome; was still impressive, with a large head so superbly bald that one couldn't imagine it contaminated by hair.

Alan was at a disadvantage because had hadn't caught the man's first name, and heard only something like "Dr. Kunis." He wasn't, he explained, a colleague of Vanessa's, but "merely a civilian member of the reading group." He was retired, had been in "private practice in town for twenty-five years." So Dr. Kunis was one of those mythical animals, the G.P. as humanist intellectual?

Alan failed to get Kunis's first name because he was distracted by Helen, who turned up at the house a minute or two after the physician. Well, here she was at last, having spent most of the day, he supposed, fuming at the hotel.

Helen hadn't been entirely alone, because Van and Josh had gone out in the afternoon to meet her at the Alexandria. Van went to cheer her sister up—she pretended it was sibling solidarity, thought Helen later, but really it was because Van's fear of confrontation meant that all arguments, even those that didn't directly concern her, had to be quickly neutralized, with the anxious extraction of promises and treaties. In the hotel lobby, where they'd had coffee as Josh's and Van's clothes dripped gray water onto the carpet, Helen protested that she'd already forgiven her father—"I've absolved him," she repeated, "I never expected any help from him anyway. I was just kind of trying it on. So, Van! You don't need to get all *nervous* about it." She told them about Alan's financial worries; neither sister had ever heard him say anything like that before. Vanessa said that their father looked "profoundly tired." The general problem, she said, was not that he gave too little, but too much.

"Why did your mom leave him, then? If that isn't a rude question?" asked Josh.

"Depends who you ask," said Van. "You know it's my weakness to see both sides of an argument."

"So I guess you only see one side of it, Helen?"

"One and a half sides, I'd say now. I spent many unproductive years blaming our mum. And the hideous Patrick Needham. Maybe as I get older I see the ways in which living with Dad must have been difficult."

"What ways?" asked Josh.

"I'd put it like this," said Helen. "All through our childhood, Van and I had numerous pets—two spaniels (male and female), two Jack Russells (also a male and a female), a cat (male), three canaries (two females and one male, or so we were told), and a couple of white rabbits (both males, as I remember). Dad fussed over those pets, complained about them, even obsessed about them, looked after them day and night, and also neglected them . . . in his own special way. And *without exception*, he called all of them 'she,' irrespective of their gender. All the time. Does that answer your question?"

"That's wicked," said Josh, with admiration.

"And not remotely fair," said Vanessa, who nevertheless had to laugh. "Though Helen's right about the animals. '*He*, Dad; not *she*; it's a *he*'—we were always having to correct him. Mummy always joked that she wanted to come back in another life as one of Dad's dogs. She thought they got superior treatment."

"He gives a lot, he withdraws a lot, he controls a lot," said Helen, with her impressive confidence. "Traits I'm faithfully replicating in my own life as a parent . . ."

"It was all a long time ago now," said Vanessa. She didn't need to add: *And besides, in the end Mummy left us in a different way.*

At the party, Helen took a brisk look at the guests in the small sitting room, and decided she would spend the evening talking to Josh and Vanessa. She felt warmly toward them for making the snowy trek to the hotel. It had been fun to spend the afternoon with her, alongside Josh as the young, eager—and slightly flirtatious!—helpmeet. Josh told Helen about his parents, his brothers, and Chicago. Helen had a sense of a powerful mind insufficiently employed; she had to stop herself, at one moment, from asking him if he wanted to come and work for her in her new venture. The two sisters—well, they could still fall into old rhythms and easy reminiscence: that day when Mum, with the girls in the back, drove the old Volvo 240 into a ditch, and was pulled out by the farmer's two massive carthorses, an absolutely magical, indelible memory for the little sisters; the afternoon when Dad broke up a fight outside the village pub and was called "a fucking wanker" by one of the men, Dad rather primly telling him to mind his language around his two young daughters; and that drab colleague of Mum's, the schoolteacher called Mr. Boggis, who started every year by saying to his new young class that his name was Rodney Boggis and they had "precisely two minutes to laugh about it," after which . . . They shared these tales with Josh, who enjoyed seeing the sisters' pleasure. The two women told only funny or eventful stories, and told them lightly, as if their mother were still alive, and living exactly where Candace Lee now occupied their childhood space.

Helen knew her father was keeping a wary eye on her; he had followed her movements as she entered the house, while he pretended to be talking to an eminent-seeming old chap with a very bald head. She wasn't angry with him, but disappointed. And determined not to show it. But she wasn't above playing a little trick on him, which occurred to her as soon as she learned from her sister that Dr. Kunis, several years retired, had once been Van's doctor.

"*Only* your doctor?" asked Helen, smiling.

"Oh—I know what you're implying, which reveals that you've never had any psychotherapy. If Dr. Kunis were my therapist, even my ex-therapist, he would *never* appear at my home, at a private event. Therapists might *wish* to meet their patients' relatives, but it's not allowed. Totally not done."

The sisters gazed at the two handsome old men, who were apparently discovering all kinds of things in common.

Helen's moment came sooner than she thought it would. She

was in the kitchen a few minutes later, talking to Josh, when Alan came in, looking—so he said—for more ice. Josh took the hint, murmured something about needing to turn down the music, and faded out of the room. Alan fussed with his bowl of ice.

"Look," he said. He was talking very quietly. "I'm excited about your new thing. There was just no need to go storming off like a bat out of darkest bloody hell at breakfast."

"I didn't go storming off. There was nothing more to talk about."

"There's plenty to talk about, but not there in public, at the hotel, and not here in public, either. When we get back to England, when we get back . . . why not come up to the house for a weekend? Bring Tom and the twins? We can talk properly about it then. I do want to help you. In any way I possibly can."

"Dad, it's okay. I've been essentially *on my own* for most of my life. I don't need any *help*. Thank you all the same."

"You were happy enough to ask for it this morning."

"*One* kind, one kind of . . . assistance. That's what we talked about at breakfast."

"*Essentially on your own?* You know you're being hurtful and completely impossible, and above all . . . extremely *unhelpful?*"

He hadn't meant to use that last word and it struck them both comically. But because they were imprisoned in their argument they were not permitted to smile, and instead lapsed into a childish, stubborn silence.

Helen was the first to crack.

"I don't want to spoil everyone's last night together, and I promised Van that I wouldn't. So I shan't. I apologize, Dad, for the thing about being on my own . . . It isn't true. It absolutely isn't true . . . You seem to be getting on brilliantly with that distinguished-looking chap."

"A nice old boy," said Alan, as if thirty years separated the two men. "He was keen to hear about my English background, seemed disappointed that I'm barely old enough to remember the war. He's a good listener, I'll say. Better than my G.P., that's for sure."

Helen couldn't help herself.

"I tried hard to get Van to admit to me that Dr. Kunis was actually her therapist and psychopharmacologist—which seems pretty obvious to me. It would explain why he's so very interested in *you*." Helen looked at her father and was inwardly delighted to see his face whiten with alarm. Poor Dad, she thought, who had a dread of all forms of surveillance.

"I may be wrong of course, it's just a strong hunch."

"Christ, Helen, why didn't Van warn me? Of course! It explains why she's so anxious around him. He's already been working on me like bloody Uri Geller—my childhood, my parents, what they did. I even told him that I got divorced. *And* all about Candace. Bloody hell."

"Just steer clear of him," said Helen.

"Oh I will, all right. Strange thing is that he seems a very nice chap, a perfectly decent bloke."

"Many therapists are, I've heard."

Alan gave his daughter suspicious scrutiny. She watched him enter the sitting room, carrying the bowl of ice, attempting to veer away from Dr. Kunis. But the room was too small; there was no protection.

27

She could smell Van's cigarette, just outside on the back porch, so she pushed open the screen door and stepped into the clear cold.

"I know I should be back inside," said Vanessa.

"It's my party, I'll be shy if I want to?"

"Okay, so I lack your strength, it would seem," said Vanessa.

"I'm not judging you. I think I'd skip your party if I were you."

"I know that by your standards a couple of academics and a doctor is pretty minor fare."

"I was joking, I was joking!"

"Sorry—I'm bloody tense. *Why* am I so tense? Wish I had something stronger in this cigarette." She flicked the butt into the dark garden. "Since we're *both* skipping out on my party, one of us must be right."

"Thanks for coming to the hotel this afternoon," said Helen. "I do like Josh. He's kind, he's bright, he's—"

"Devilishly handsome?"

"Angelically? Still too young to be devilishly—lucky chap."

"He is my absolute love, Helen," she said with simple pride. "I love him."

"And I can see why." For a second, she felt pettily envious, and almost added: *the whole town can probably tell you're in love.*

"The *only* thing we ever argue about is my smoking . . . I think I want to go back to England with him."

"I said to Dad this morning that you should be teaching at Oxford or London, or somewhere like that, not out here."

"I want to show him off there!"

"Does he want to go? He strikes me as quite American."

"Two months ago I would have said no. *Now* I think he does."

Having some idea of what had happened in the last two months, Helen suddenly felt very sorry for her sister; it took her breath away.

"Have you and Dad made up?" asked Van. "I could see you in the kitchen—I looked through the window. It all looked terribly serious. You know he'll come through in the end. He's just treating your proposal like a deal. Dangling you, a bit."

"I really don't need him anyway."

"It's partly a matter of dragging him, kicking and screaming, into the future—away from his own projects. Josh and I were talking about it last night. You're a utopian. Always on the move, restless . . . I feel very stuck here, by contrast. Old, snagged on my old books."

"Oh, you love your books. They're your best friends. You do have an awful lot, though . . . Three thousand?"

"Probably around that."

"Dad and I agreed to differ. But I played a little joke on him, I couldn't help it. I suggested to him that the good doctor is actually your therapist."

"So *that's* where you were heading . . ."

"He's trying very hard to avoid him—as we speak."

"Surprise, surprise—Dad knows as little about therapeutic protocol as you do. It would *never* happen." But Vanessa was smiling, and her eyes were bright. She'd always been somewhat in awe of her sister's boldness. "It would be like inviting to dinner the judge who is deciding on your very delicate court case."

"Now don't go and spoil it by whispering the truth in his ear," said Helen.

"You *are* wicked, just as Josh said . . ."

28

In the sitting room, Alan was clinking an ice cube into his Scotch, his back to the room, when he was taken by surprise. Josh was right behind him, almost talking into his ear.

"Alan, sorry by the way if it seemed we were ganging up on you last night. If it's a consolation, to go back to our conversation, there are a bunch of things that computers can't do, may never be able to do in my opinion. Yeah, Deep Blue beat Kasparov in 1997. So what? A computer can store more data about possible chess moves than humans ever could. But computers can't beat humans at poker or Go. So it ain't *the end of the world as we know it*. Not *yet*, anyway."

Josh, in his way, was trying to be kind. But why do I need "consolation"? How weak does he take me to be? Do I act as if I think it's the end of the world? He found himself standing in Van's living room, once Josh had moved away, doing some furious mental computation of his own—to be precise, fighting the American War of Independence all over again. The Battle of Saratoga, but this time with General Burgoyne triumphant, not defeated, and using very different weapons. This young American, who looked only forward, not backward, who seemed able to discard everything that had produced who Alan was, and everything that Alan had produced . . . Well, let's see how he'd actually get on in the modern world, without the British contribution.

Gravity—Newton!—electricity—Faraday!—circulation of the blood—Harvey!—evolution—Darwin!—antisepsis—Lister!—penicillin—Fleming!—the steam engine—Trevithick!—the steam turbine (especially dear to him because that was where his dad had worked)—Parsons!—the atom—Rutherford!—the jet engine—Whittle!—the computer—Turing!—DNA—Crick! Or was it Watson? The English one, anyway. The modern age *is* British. Or was. Without any of that, without the country he so easily flicked aside, Josh would be a diseased, immobile caveman.

Dr. Kunis approached Alan, and hesitated. But it was too late, because Alan was staring at him—with a rather sickly look on his face, thought Kunis.

"Parties have exactly the same effect on me," he said very charmingly.

"Oh, I'm fine with parties. Really I am," Alan said quickly.

"That's not how you looked."

"How did I look?" asked Alan, all indifference. He expected Kunis to say something like "You looked like a lost child, as if you were reliving your childish fears of being abandoned by your mother," and was relieved when the distinguished guest said, "You looked slightly annoyed, as if you haven't been able to get exactly the *right* drink this evening."

"That's absolutely true, in fact."

He told Dr. Kunis that he had to go upstairs for a minute: "nature calls." And he quickly left the room, avoiding the lavatory behind the kitchen, climbing swiftly the loud, uncarpeted, cream-painted staircase. Kunis had blown it by asking Alan, once again, about his childhood in Durham. Good lord, he wasn't going to stand here in Van's house and be psyched out by his daughter's own therapist. He didn't need to pee, but went through the motions anyway, quietly entering the bathroom next to Van and Josh's bedroom, locking the door behind him, and pointlessly standing in front of the lavatory. He hadn't been in this room. It was modest. And not especially clean—the result of a couple whose higher-order occupations put dirt well below their notice. Sink, console, taps, and lavatory were all of the cheapest kind: the tap was one of those push-pull things topped by a crimped diamantine plastic disc; cheap as hell but hideously indestructible—the washers went on for years. Van's long dark hairs were on the floor, in the sink, and clogged her large, upturned porcupine hairbrush; he thought of how, at home, the sheep left their cloudy white wool on the barbed wire fences. The underside of the lavatory seat was dotted with blurred yellowish stains. Josh's dried piss. And Alan imagined Van, rushed and careless, spending two minutes on her knees with bleach and a cloth every once in a while, because although she didn't care very much about such things, it *was* getting a bit *revolting*, and Josh never did *anything* around the house (of that Alan was absolutely sure)—and when this harried domestic picture came to him, he had a surge of compassion. Van!—he suddenly remembered Candace's advice, and bent to look under the sink. Nothing there. The flimsy door closed with a cheap snap. Perhaps above the sink? He opened what was almost certainly an IKEA cabinet. Male stuff on the right—shaving foam, razors, deodorant. Female on the left? There was a pill cylinder, made out of an unfamiliar smoked-orange plastic, with a kind of white flywheel cap marked CVS. This was it. "Vanessa Querry. Bupropion (Wellbutrin). 0.5 mg." The bottle was half-full. He committed the name to memory—certain that he would eventually get *p* confused with *b*—and flushed the toilet. It swallowed sluggishly, without much appetite; he wondered how it could possibly do its business when called upon to transfer Josh's heavy crap.

Downstairs, guests were starting to leave. Dr. Kunis was already in the hall. The air was close, odorous, as if invisibly dropleted with alcohol. Alan was sorry he hadn't spoken more to Vanessa's colleagues. Perhaps he would see them in the next few days? Not Gary Mulhall: he was flying tomorrow—"weather willing"—to Austin, Texas, to give a paper at a two-day conference. Amy Isaacson said she would be around "on campus," but said it in such a way that made very clear—without rudeness, Alan noted admiringly—she would have little time for Professor Querry's aged old pa. By contrast Dr. Kunis had the ample hours of the elderly retiree: he would be delighted to see Alan again; he lived only three blocks away; Vanessa had all his details. In response, Alan tried to warn him off, with some of Amy Isaacson's style, but succeeded only in seeming peculiar, even a little hostile.

Once the door had closed—ghosts of dead polar air clinging to them in the crowded hallway—Vanessa turned to her father and said, gently, "So, Dad, did you not like Theo Kunis?"

"Well, Vanessa, I think I have the right not to be psychoanalyzed by my own daughter's therapist. I'm surely to blame for a great deal, but not for everything."

"Oh, here we go! Daddy, he's not a therapist or psychoanalyst, he's never been one, though I know he's read a lot of Freud. He was a doctor in town for twenty-plus years. My G.P., and Amy's, too. Now retired. That's the only connection. That and the reading group."

"Is that true? Really?" He felt foolish. "Why did Helen claim he was your therapist, then?"

"I didn't *claim* he was," said Helen. "I didn't know. I *suspected* he was." She was smiling slightly, teeth showing.

"I think you were trying to wind me up, Helen. I don't appreciate being tricked like that."

For the rest of the evening, until she finally got Josh to drive them back to the hotel, Vanessa enjoyed playing parent—playing mum—to her warring father and sister. If they wouldn't keep the peace, she would have to enforce it.

29

As Vanessa saw it—she sat for a while on the sofa, smoking a cigarette as she waited for Josh to return from the Alexandria—her sister and father were condemned to quarrel. They were both proud, impulsive people who considered themselves largely modest and rational. When she was younger, she sometimes envied Helen for the fierce arguments she got into with their parents. When Dad and Helen argued, they were having a conversation of equals, were at least honoring some kind of emotional contract, two confident temperaments who had decided that the matter at stake was truly *at stake*; that life was action and not only reflection; that a position could be won, not just intellectually but emotionally. Vanessa hated confrontation—partly because she couldn't believe that anyone who had strongly argued with her could ever like her again.

Besides, didn't arguments always come a beat too late? They were like thunder, chasing the lightning strike of anger; noisy tributes to an energy that had already dissipated. And another problem was that she could all too easily detach herself from the issue at hand and see that it was—*sub specie aeternitatis*—about nothing very much. Was this detachment in fact a "problem"? Was it what was sometimes called "a fatal detachment"? Did it stop her living properly? On the contrary, she was passionate about many things, and about some things she was more passionate than her younger sister. Surely she missed Mum more fiercely than Helen ever did, for instance? Perhaps that was because she had been alone for so long, with no partner or children for comfort or distraction. In her solitude, Vanessa had desperately longed for her mother. She would wake up day after day, having seen Mummy in blessed dreams, forced by her visions to relive the scandal of her death. A simple, wailing, childlike question filled her being—one, she understood, both unphilosophical and the most philosophical question anyone could ask: "Where has she gone?" It was astonishing, unfathomable, that she had simply vanished. The woman who, when she entered any room, made it *smell* like her—her beautiful, particular fragrance. In Northumberland, there was a grave, and a body—well, a meal of bones—which she could visit. But where had her mother's spirit gone? She wanted to be able to believe in the afterlife of her mother's spirit, would joyfully have communicated with its presence in some Buddhist way. There was memory, which was everything of course; there was Helen, who so resembled, in certain moments, their mother, and who even *smelled* just like her. And there was the grave in the north of England with its sunken, ravaged, earthbound receipt. But there was nothing else. No spirit. Not even in the church in Malta, where her neighbors spoke so easily about "conquering death." She had disappeared. And poor Mummy! Why should *she* be in the ground while Daddy thrived? With Candace.

She couldn't bear to think these thoughts, and couldn't stop either. This was her real "problem"—not detachment but its opposite. In recent years, Vanessa had come to the conclusion that the strengths one needed as an academic philosopher had dismayingly little to do with how she lived her life. In philosophy, you had to keep thinking relentlessly, to examine and reexamine, until you came to a stop. That stop, that cessation of argument, was formal rather than actual, intellectual rather than metaphysical. Still, it was helpful. You reached the limit of the designated

argument, the end of the length of string you had already selected: the essay had to end, the paper was finally delivered to its
audience, the lecture course finished. The professional philosopher usually gestured to wilder and deeper areas of thought, unfinished and perhaps unfinishable complexities, but these lay
beyond the formal boundaries of the lecture, the essay, the book.
She had decided to become a philosopher after reading—no,
while reading—Thomas Nagel's essay on "The Absurd." She still
had the notes she made: Oxford, 1986. And there was no better
example of purposeful examination, and knowing where to stop
examining things, than *that* essay. Nagel knew how to think; and
when to stop thinking.

His essay spoke to Vanessa because it spoke calmly (that is to
say, philosophically) about metaphysical meaninglessness. Nagel
laid out a series of concentric circles: it is natural, he conceded, to
step back from the purpose of one's individual life and doubt its
point; it is natural to ask: Why am I doing what I am doing?
What is the meaning and design of my life? And natural to wonder: perhaps it *has no* purpose or design. And outside this circle
there is a further, larger circle of doubt: in like manner, we can
also step back from all of human history, or from the entire progress of science, or from society or politics, or from the very globe
itself, and ask: So what? What does any of this little mundane
struggle amount to? What is its design and purpose? And also to
wonder: perhaps it *has no* purpose or design. Everything, says
Nagel, seen under the eye of eternity, can be "put into question,"
and when we do so, we stand on the brink of the Absurd, we stare
into the abyss. Vanessa remembered reading this essay as a
twenty-year-old, and furiously underlining those cool, hard sentences, and admiring the acute, even tread of the thought, and
nodding in passionate agreement. But then Nagel played the academic philosopher, and closed his argument, finished his brief
paper, which was obviously a tightly repressed argument with
Camus. We shouldn't worry too much about the Absurd, Nagel

concluded, because if under the eye of eternity, nothing matters, then under the eye of eternity the Absurd doesn't matter either—"and we can approach our absurd lives with irony instead of heroism or despair."

And young Vanessa sat up—she was reading the essay in bed, in her drafty room at New College—disagreeing violently, and felt that she wanted to quarrel on paper with Thomas Nagel, and that this wanting to quarrel on paper, not in person but on paper, was a philosophical urge. Logically, Nagel was impeccable: if nothing matters, then indeed nothing matters *at all*, including one's despair about the fact that nothing matters. But all the same!—how *could* one, having worked so expertly through the premises of Camus's eloquent argument in *The Myth of Sisyphus*, a book she adored, just turn around and calmly ignore those premises? For if nothing matters, then philosophy doesn't matter, either. The tenured professor from New York University told the uninsured, passionate Frenchman (a heroic figure but not, as Sartre sniffed, much of a philosopher), a man who had lived through the Second World War and the Algerian War, that getting *too* worked up about the Absurd was a little . . . *absurd*. Better to be ironic, self-aware, coolly analytical, than passionate or despairing.

She saw, now, that her own small battle to reconcile analytic philosophy and continental European philosophy could probably be traced back to this moment, in bed in her Oxford college . . . Sartre was right: Camus was no great philosopher. But Vanessa admired Camus for *not* being philosophically sophisticated. Now she felt that Nagel stood for academic philosophy, with all its strengths and weaknesses, and that Camus was *life*, with all its bigger strengths and bigger weaknesses. It was easy to go on functioning and drawing a good salary if one performed according to Nagel. But it was harder to go on functioning if one lived according to Camus, and perhaps this was why she had not prospered in the academic field. It was clearly dangerous to spend too much time, in life, reflecting *on* life. If one knew *how to think and then how to stop thinking,* how to open and close the circle of thought, one flourished in life—and in that division of it known as academic philosophy. But what if one's series of circles just kept on multiplying? What if it was hard to stop thinking about pointlessness, to stop thinking about metaphysical absurdity, to stop thinking about the brevity and meaninglessness of things? What if despair—awful, awful despair—kept on returning, precisely because one could not, like Nagel, put it "into question"?

Josh—Josh *put a stop* to her solitude, put a stop to her excessive reflection, her abysmal sense that nothing was really worth living for. (*You swallow the universe like a pill, but then you piss it out, too, it passes out of you, along with everything else important.*) She loved Josh so much. She loved him, for . . . where to start? For having a body . . . Start there. Maybe a foolish way of putting it, except that her other boyfriends, such as they were (all two of them!), had been almost ethereal by contrast: embarrassed to have bodies at all. Josh liked his, and was insistent with it. She loved that insistence, the presence of his need, which quickly stoked need in her. She loved his strong arms, she liked to feel his selfish cock pushing against her leg, loved the way he closed his eyes and frowned, as if in deep thought, when he was about to come. When she was with Josh, everything—all *this*—came to a stop. And how she hated waking, to find that he had already risen; then everything—all *this*—started up again.

It had all "started up again" three months ago. Worse than the very worst times in her life. At dinner one evening, she had done no more than suggest that she and Josh might move, at some vague point in the future, to England for a while—she'd had enough of Skidmore, she said she was tired of the fifteen American flags bragging from various buildings along Broadway. And Josh got an awful, shifty, uncomfortable look on his face, and she knew, just *knew* . . . something terrible. He would never come to England with her.

She could endure that. Fine, they would live in Saratoga Springs—or New York, or Chicago. Wherever he wanted. What she could not endure, could not bear to think about but could not stop thinking about, was the void that opened up when Josh got that shifty, smiling, weak, wary look: the idea that he couldn't contemplate coming to England, not because he could not imagine living in that country, but because he could not imagine living anywhere with her in the future. Josh was a child, really. He lived in an eternal present, with very few things—a drawer of T-shirts and underwear, and a laptop. She loved this carelessness. It was morally admirable, too: *consider the lilies*. He rarely looked ahead, gave little "thought for the morrow"; and at that moment when she asked him to, he retreated from her, with a foolish, grinning weakness on his handsome face.

The anguish was indescribable. She couldn't sleep. At night, Josh lay next to her in bed, extinct, like the corpse of their relationship. In the mornings, she couldn't get out of bed, either. She could barely drag herself through her classes. So Josh left her, gave up on her really, went back to Chicago to visit his parents, and Vanessa canceled her ticket to go home to Northumberland for Christmas, and she still could not sleep, but she could not really rise either, and Dr. Lasky prescribed Wellbutrin, which did nothing. She wanted her father and sister to come and rescue her, but was too ashamed to tell them what was wrong; she wanted her mother to be alive, wanted Mummy to visit her bedside (Lucozade and grapes) as she used to when little Vanny got sick. She lay in that bed, immobilized, utterly daunted by the day. Just the prospect of showering, or having to make breakfast, or phoning Josh in Chicago, seemed an immense task. Her right arm began to hurt, she could barely lift it, there was some kind of paralysis, and one morning she went into the bathroom, and looked at herself in the mirror, and was very afraid that she was going to wound her arm. Barely an hour later, she fell down the

stairs and broke that very arm—and then at last the Wellbutrin
began to work.

The accident changed everything, as physical wounds generally did. The neighbors, the evangelical Christians who lived
next door, heard her cry out and rigged up a sling for her, and
drove her to the ER. She phoned Josh, and he returned immediately from Chicago, and was solicitous, attentive. Remorseful. He
made a card, faced with a photograph of them both, taken very
early in their relationship by Amy Isaacson; inside it, he wrote,
sweetly, awkwardly: "England, the U.K., Europe, the World, the
Universe. Wherever you want." Josh was suddenly different.
He was engaged with her, he told her stories about his parents,
and insisted that she go back with him to Chicago for the
Christmas break, to meet them.

On Christmas Day in Chicago, they ate Chinese takeout (no
turkey, no Brussels sprouts boiled into ragged submission). Josh's
parents seemed to like Vanessa, and she couldn't help liking
them. They were intellectuals, for one thing. She loved the large,
comfortable apartment, mad with books, and its grand view
of the shifting acreage of Lake Michigan. And it was a happy
house. You could tell these things pretty quickly; homes emitted
their qualities like an odor. The household, then, was a good ad-
vertisement for Josh's mother, who was a family psychiatrist.
Vanessa liked that the setup was a matriarchy—Josh and his
father deferred to Wendy Rich, were tender and solicitous. She,
in turn, was calm and even-tempered. Josh got his looks from his
mum: Vanessa thought she was beautiful, long-faced and elegant.
She flinched at first from Wendy, fearing that the professional
therapist was always at work, diagnosing and analyzing. When
Wendy stared at her, Vanessa quickly looked away, in order to
protect her soul. How much had Josh told his mother? What did
she make of the cast on her right arm? But Wendy Rich was
much more interested in children than in adults. It was child

development that fascinated her. She said that as far as she was concerned, it was "all over" by the age of ten—or was it twelve? Wendy was impressed by Vanessa's profession, and wanted to engage her in discussion about the philosophers she had read at Columbia in the late 1960s—Marcuse, Arendt, Sartre. Vanessa did her best, but felt she underperformed.

Josh's father, Adam Rich, had several of his son's mannerisms: he spoke fast, with a slight lisp, and he had the same adhesive way with obscure facts. But Adam was worldlier than Josh, more interested in success and fine things. He enjoyed his many "gadgets," and showed them off to Vanessa: the Nespresso machine ("best two hundred dollars I ever spent"), the stainless-steel juicer, the odd contraption whose function was to remove a wine cork in three seconds. Adam sometimes reminded Vanessa of her father. She thought the two men would like each other. Then she decided that Adam Rich might intimidate Alan Querry, who was intimidated by very little, except by precisely Adam's strengths: intellectual fluency, and a kind of confidence that in America was Jewish but which in England would have been aristocratic.

Above all, she liked the way that Adam and Wendy spoke to each other. Unlike her own parents (so she remembered), they had learned how to tease each other without arguing. Adam's great treasure—his best gadget—was a small boat he kept in the 31st Street Harbor. Wendy complained to Vanessa that he never took it out on the water. "If you added up all the times he's used it and divided that into the cost of keeping it, you'd have a dismal figure." Yes, said Adam genially, "but if I divided all the times I *think* about it into the cost, then the figure would look a lot better."

It was on her third day in Chicago that Vanessa understood that she wanted to be part of this intellectual but worldly family, and live in their house forever. She noticed, on a side table, one of Wendy's psychology books, which had an absurd title: *Gender as*

Soft Assembly ("it's newish—and very good, in fact," said Wendy).
The title became one of those small, silly things that a group
laughs about. Josh deliberately worked it into his sentences—
"when my brothers are home, it's more like gender as hard assembly," and so on—and when at some moment around the table
they started laughing once more at the ridiculous *Gender as Soft
Assembly*, she became aware that she wasn't full of despair. Surrounded by these warm people, encouraged also by the air of
holiday truancy—by the fact that it was Christmas outside but
not Christmas inside this house—her sadness seemed to lift
somewhat. That was Josh's gift to her: over Jewish Christmas, he
gave her his family.

And he did more. After the trip to Chicago, they went back
to Saratoga Springs and talked about what lay ahead, and about
what life in England might be like, and then he e-mailed Helen
and suggested that if she were visiting New York anytime soon,
she should come upstate and raise her sister's spirits. Helen, of
course, then spoke to Dad, so that it was Josh who was directly
responsible—for better or worse!—for Dad's first visit to her house
in Saratoga Springs.

But despair was never banished; the memory, and therefore
the prospect of it, always lurked. She was often put in mind of a
childhood holiday she had taken in Cornwall, and her strange,
uncanny sense that the blue thrill of the sea was always nearby.
Within the corridors of high hedgerows, the funneled lanes, you
could feel the sea just beyond, and how the land continued and
then stopped, and broke into cliff. In every field, every road, you
had that knowledge—of the infinite dashing restlessness of sea,
just out of sight, at the end of everything. Magical and a bit terrifying, was how she remembered it. But the image was differently
terrifying, humiliating even, for a forty-year-old philosopher
who regularly lectured on "Aristotle and human flourishing."
For despair was like a sea. It threshed restlessly, just out of sight,

always there: the deep enemy of human flourishing, inching
away at its borders. For now, she had pushed away that sadness
(but make sure you keep on taking your Wellbutrin, said
Dr. Lasky). Happier than she'd been for a long time, she had
some reason to hope that Josh's foolish, wary smile had been ig-
norantly fearful rather than knowingly fatalistic. He seemed so
different now.

30

At the hotel, Alan rose early the next morning to get in a phone call to Candace, who gave specialist information about the Wellbutrin—an antidepressant, commonly prescribed to treat anxiety, insomnia, mood swings, and so on.

"But *why* is she depressed?" cried Alan, in childish frustration. "Is that really a helpful approach, love?"

Was there another, more serious drug, Candy asked, that she might be taking? She thought that Vanessa was almost certainly on at least two forms of medication. If she were *your* daughter, he thought to himself, you wouldn't want to confirm the existence of a second drug; you would have to look away from the subject; your gaze would turn to ashes. Instead he told her—it was true—that he felt he'd been away "forever." It was the snow that locked him into this icy white kingdom; or the intensity of his emotions, which made him frail, despite the brave face he turned to the world. Time seemed to trudge by slowly here in heavy snow boots. Candy gave him news and gossip from home, to cheer him up: their neighbor the Baronet (a word she found movingly hard to pronounce) was going to build an indoor swimming pool, because of Lady Compton's terrible arthritis—the swimming might help. Alan loved these stories, was easily soothed by them. Right now, the Baronet's life seemed ideal, an existence of perfect, unreflective Englishness. But he didn't have time to listen to more,

he had to speak to his mother, too. And Mam had stories also—
one involved an old lady at the Home who'd been working for
years on a sacred tapestry for her church and had finally finished
it, only to discover that the diocese was now closing and decom-
missioning the little church—which predictably did the opposite
of soothing him. Mam wanted to hear everything about Josh.
Did he look like the photograph Van had sent her? Was he "a
nice young man"? Couldn't Vanessa marry him and move back
home? Van was old but not so old that she couldn't have at least
one child. Nowadays women in their forties were having children
all the time, "in the newspapers." She had not the faintest idea
about Vanessa's life in Saratoga, but still she was like Mr. Bridger
in *The Italian Job*, running Italian operations from his English
prison cell, thought Alan wearily as he put the phone down. Yet
when he heard his mother's voice, he wanted to be sitting next to
her as she sat in the old chintz chair. Long, long ago, when she
came upstairs to kiss him goodnight, he would ask her: "Have
you brought your knitting?" And when she said yes, he was
pleased, because it meant that Mam would stay and tell him a
story.

•

They all had breakfast together at Vanessa's. Helen, who was
leaving in an hour for New York, and then for London, was powerful, straight-backed, almost embarrassingly vital. She praised her
elder sister for rather slight accomplishments: "Fabulous coffee,
Van, thanks so much! Whose jam is this? Local, aha. Well *done*
on finding it." Alan knew what was up: she was atoning for her
excitement at leaving. Van was subdued, anxious, otherworldly,
slouching. She was teaching her first class of the term, at twelve
o'clock, on ethics and action, and didn't feel prepared; she had
brought a book to the table. She made a wan joke about having
to lecture "to the lucky kids at Lucy Skidmore Scribner's Young

Women's Industrial Club" (the college's original name, it turned out).

Alan had forgotten that Vanessa would have to go out and earn a living, just like everyone else. And Josh—he stood near the toaster, bouncing slightly on the balls of his feet and sneezing. He had some kind of morning allergy. And there was a new T-shirt: CHILMARK F.D. KEEP BACK 300 FEET. Alan was happy to follow that particular order. "How many do you have?" he asked, pointing toward Josh's chest. "Oh, you ain't seen nothin' yet," Josh replied cheerfully.

Helen's car arrived early, of course—a gigantic black Chevy Suburban, menacing and funereal, the thick exhaust gurgling like a boat's. A smartly dressed Latino driver, small alongside his glossed black barge, held the rear door open. Inside, cream leather seats, and dashboard fans raging with hot air. American abundance: Helen loved it. She'd paid for a driver to take her the three and a half hours to New York. Farewells were brief and intense. Alan hugged Helen fiercely, gratefully kissing her Cathy-like neck, inhaling her Cathy-like scent—he wanted her to know, by this gesture, that he had no anger. In his line of work, there were two types of builders: the shouters, the big bullies; and the patient, quiet ones. The ones who rode out the storms. He knew which type he was. Helen promised to call when she was back in London. She and Vanessa embraced, and Helen appeared to whisper something in her sister's ear. The slab-cheeked Chevy crunched down the drive, the brake lights appeared brightly, and she was gone.

Some sort of embarrassment overcame them as they sat down again in the kitchen—the embarrassment of nudity, of revelation: they had lost their covering. Without Helen, what on earth would they say to each other? Salvation: the weekend was over, it was Monday morning and time to work. Josh said he had to go into town to scan something, and to print something else out in color. Vanessa would leave shortly for the campus, where she was meeting with students, and then had her noon lecture. Was Dad interested in lunch, after that? Back at the house? What would he do until then? Alan thought he would stay put for a while, have some more coffee, read *The New York Times*. And then, since Van and Josh were bound to be busy over the next few days, perhaps he would see about hiring a car. He wanted to drive around a bit, explore the surrounding area—the famous "upstate New York." It would keep him occupied. Vanessa said he should take her car, the Toyota. Because of the arm, she couldn't use it anyway. Alan had been secretly looking forward to driving a lordly American boat with a flabby V8, but he accepted Van's generous— and economical—offer. Rising, Josh said he would walk with Vanessa over to the college. She started clearing up the plates. "Leave that to me," said Alan, "I'm on the personal equivalent of island time. You go and get ready for class." He enjoyed hearing her run upstairs, the exasperated sighs, the banging of the bathroom door. Like old days, with the girls preparing for school . . .

31

He was on his own, reading *The New York Times*—he liked the newspaper's obituaries: in America they actually told you *what* the subject had died of, instead of that English euphemism "after a long illness" (which he knew from personal experience to be no euphemism anyway)—and was thinking about leaving when the doorbell rang. Surely it wasn't Josh, back already from town and temporarily locked out. But there was a complete stranger at the freezing door—a bland-looking middle-aged man, chiefly notable for his lack of a coat.

"I'm Jerry Dent—we met on Saturday evening, but it was dark. We live right next door. The dog . . ."

"Yes—*yes*. Alan. Afraid Vanessa's at work. Back at lunchtime."

"In fact I'd like to have a quick word with you, if you have a moment. Would you mind?" He was solicitous, forceful, mild, all at once. Alan knew the style: local vicar. Wary but helpless, he felt he had to invite the man into the kitchen. He was taller than Jerry, and stronger, he reckoned, despite their difference in years. If it should come to that . . . Jerry was shoulderless as a beaver, with a vague soft middle. Unmuscular Christianity. Alan thanked him for helping Vanessa when she fell down the stairs.

"She told me that you and your wife made a sling—with a tea towel!—and drove her to the hospital. That was really very kind. I can tell you, I don't have any neighbors like that where I live."

"It was the least we could do . . . She was . . . well, she was in pretty bad shape when we found her. I don't just mean physically. To be honest, this is what I came to talk to you about—I saw that Josh and Vanessa left the house this morning, that you were alone, so I came on over . . . Diane and I are very concerned about Vanessa. I have the sense"—Jerry looked around, theatrically—"of a house that is not at unity with itself. I get a real sense of sadness here, of *spiritual* sadness."

"Well," said Alan, strangely moved, "over the years, poor Vanessa's been through the wars. Like her sister. Like all of us— death, divorce, and taxes."

Jerry was single-minded. "But who's going to lead her out of the wars? Who'll save her?" he asked.

"Now what does that mean? I know I'm only here for a week or so, but I am trying to make myself useful."

"Do not put your trust in princes, in mortal man . . ."

"Sorry?"

"I'm not reproaching you. *What* will save her? Vanessa came to our church in Malta, you know. She said she was there just to 'observe' things, but she didn't act like a neutral observer."

"No? How so?" Alan was interested.

"During one of the testimonials, she knelt down and started crying. We were sitting right next to her. A lot of pain was inside her, we thought, and also sin. It was really the sin coming out of her that made her cry like that."

"Pain, but not sin," said Alan firmly. "Not sin."

Jerry smiled. "You're very sure about sinlessness. Good for you. Christians can't be so certain."

"I'm not certain about *my* lack of sin, just about hers." Alan also wanted to say: just bloody well leave her out of it. "And as far as I know," he continued, "Vanessa isn't a Christian. Not yet."

"Maybe not, but she came a second time to the church, and

spent most of *that* service praying. Praying intensely. Eyes tightly
shut. Praying to someone or something. Point is—she needs something to lead her out of her pain. And it sure won't be secular
drugs."

"Drugs . . ."

Jerry seemed impatient.

"When we took her to the hospital, she had to tell the nurse
at the desk if she was allergic to anything, and if she was taking
any prescription medication at the time. Diane was standing
next to her, and saw Vanessa write down the name of two different antidepressant—"

"That's *her* business, it *must* be her own business. Is that
clear?"

"Clear, clear. Clear as navy coffee, as my old man used to say.
Okay, wait: I didn't come here to fight or make you mad. We're
just concerned about our neighbor. I'm very sorry if I've given
you bad news . . . But I have a responsibility, as a Christian . . .
Alan, would you—would you mind if I pray with you? I'd like
to do *that*."

He minded intensely, but didn't want to seem unreasonable—
after all, Van would have to live side by side with these God-
botherers, practically sitting in the same pew as them, well after he
had gone. Jerry, very unexpectedly, took Alan's hand, and lowered
his head. It was like having to say grace again at meals, as a kid,
when all your instincts were to giggle or kick your best friend's
shins under the table. Just like a compliant kid, astounded he
was doing this—and aware suddenly that he needed to pee—he
closed his eyes. Jerry's hand was dry. His loose body centered itself,
and shook slightly. His voice seemed to take on quivering depth,
like an Elvis impersonator: casino basso.

"Lord Jesus, we ask for your blessing on this house, and on
all who live and stay within it. We offer up this servant, Vanessa,
and this servant, Alan, for your blessing and protection, so that
you may turn strife into concord, and dry soil into fertile land.

That you may *heal* Vanessa, Lord. Above all, we pray, Lord, that the gift of your serenity may descend upon this house, mindful of the example of your supreme sacrifice, certain in the knowledge that the greatest serenity can come only from you, our Savior, Jesus Christ. Amen."

"Amen," said Alan strongly. As prayers go, it—had gone: he'd expected far worse. Jerry looked at him with optimistic surprise, as if the pretty girl at the party had unexpectedly agreed to dance with him. *Fishers of men, fishers of men*, thought Alan.

Once Jerry had left, Alan, feeling a bit dazed, decided he must quickly leave the house. He couldn't bear encountering Josh. Wonderfully, terrifyingly, he had no plans—the day was as wide open as a snowy prairie. He had a vague idea that he would drive around a bit, check out the terrain. It was beautiful out there—depthless blue sky, irradiated by the white of the ground—but it was too cold to walk far. So he clicked himself into Van's Prius, smiling as he noticed four academic library books scattered across the backseat. The Toyota Prius really was a vile machine: he understood that it was a hybrid vehicle, but did it also have to look like an amphibious one? Ugly front lights, like most modern vehicles. When he was growing up, cars had human faces—wide mouths and round eyes set far apart. The old Rover P5B looked eerily like Harold Wilson, which perhaps explained why the prime minister had always used one. So the silly girl smoked in her car—the thickened, trapped air was almost intolerable at first. Like the old smoking carriages on the trains, or the top floor of the double-decker buses. The ashtray and console were powdered with gray cigarette ash, and twisted fag ends filled the tray; there were two old water bottles, rolling around in the front passenger well; the seat fabric was torn in a couple of places; something had been spilled on the backseat. A box of antibacterial wipes, jammed into the driver's door bin, offered a chimera of correction.

He drove down Broadway, past the fabulous Alexandria, past

the fine buildings, and slowly out of town. All the better if he could get off the main road, into the fields and back lanes. Where the life is. You drive on the bloody *right* here, he said to himself. *Links fahren. Tenez la gauche*—no, that's Dover, coming *back* from France. A little nervously he fell behind a line of cars. Another Prius was directly in front of him, bright purple, its rear gummed with stickers like a student's rucksack. AT LEAST THE WAR AGAINST GLOBAL WARMING IS GOING WELL. THE RAPTURE IS NOT AN EXIT STRATEGY. W STANDS FOR WAR. I'M ALREADY AGAINST THE NEXT WAR. It was exhausting, in the way of Josh's shirts, though he was smiling.

When the tattooed Prius turned left, off the main road, he did the same, slowing down to adjust to the smaller road. He was passing bare wintry fields, and was in farming country, or so it seemed—a church-like barn, silvery silos standing upright like missiles. A quad bike with a trailer. The road had no verge; a foolhardy pedestrian would have to make do with a grassy ditch. But the countryside never stopped being urban: a big modern high school came and went (GO KNIGHTS); there were petrol stations, and some kind of veterans' hall (CHICKEN DINNER, MONDAY); a beaten-up Ford pickup truck for sale, ninety-two thousand miles, parked in the middle of a vast, clean, snowy front lawn, like one of those brutal modern poems self-consciously surrounded by a lot of white page; an unconvincing motel—tiny, low wooden cabins somewhat resembling veal hutches—that seemed likely to have closed in 1957, but which still advertised vacancies; a shack whose hanging sign offered geeks' help for computer problems (Only Connect, the business was called). For miles and miles, so it seemed, the spoiled enterprising landscape persisted—or subsisted, thought Alan, for it was clear enough, clear as navy coffee indeed, that outside Saratoga Springs, life was extremely difficult, hard, austerely poor in a way that strongly reminded him of North East England and his childhood: how he and his parents wore everything out to extinction, how he and Mam walked *everywhere* (those smoky Newcastle streets). Before they moved to Durham—and moved up in the world—Mam pretended to the fancy neighbors at the end of the street, in the big corner house, that they ate meat at least three times a week for dinner. The old dirty-laundry smell of boiled cabbage: to this day, he refused to eat cabbage, refused to buy it. And yet he liked what he saw here. It was distinct, everything had sharp outlines, the shock of its difference had its own kind of strong pewter taste.

He wanted to drive to Troy, to see what Helen had been talking about, but he turned back because an idea had formed—to get to the campus and watch Vanessa's lecture, which began in forty minutes or so. He turned round, accelerated, insofar as that was possible in a Prius, and got back to town in half an hour.

32

Skidmore's campus had the pleasant woodsy feel of Saratoga generally, as if the students were at university to study forestry: all these wonderful trees, rootless in the high snow—the thick maples, the tall nude poplars (nothing looked more abandoned than a poplar in winter), the slender silver birches with their tattered, wounded-looking bark. Too many car parks, the besetting American sin; but he used one of them now, pointed toward it by a helpful student (he had had to suppress the inclination to ask, "You're not also on your way to Professor Querry's lecture?"), and entered an anonymous-looking brick building with deeply recessed window frames. Up the functional staircase, through a series of plain doors, and he was at last in the philosophy department. Well, what had he expected—the Parthenon? Trinity College, Cambridge? It was very small, barely larger than the village post office at home. At what seemed to be a reception desk or secretarial outpost, he asked where he might find Professor Querry's noon lecture. "You mean 'Introduction to Ethics: Action and Reflection'? You're in the community auditors' program?" Alan said that he was. Then you go through the door, down the corridor, and turn right. Just look for the Ballston Room. He was nervous like a child, he could feel his arms trembling as he walked along the corridor; a student pushed past him. The kid was going to the same place—to a room that resembled the interior of a church, with long, banked, semi-circular desks. Alan scanned the place for an unobtrusive seat. At the back, top row, next to the only other old person in the room, who was presumably legitimately enrolled in the community auditors' program. Who was—ah, Dr. Kunis . . . stylish and elfin in a green woolen cap. An elegant green elf. Of course. Alan despaired for a second, then reminded himself that Dr. Kunis was not in fact a therapist, and that Alan had been inexplicably curt with him in the last minutes of their previous encounter. With warmth he gripped the outstretched hand, and pretended to be fulfilling a long-standing engagement: to come and listen to his daughter lecture. Who entered now, down the stairs, papers in hand. Alan had a schoolboy's instinct to rise to his feet (Old World Kunis would understand that impulse, surely); he tried to control his shameful anxiety, his wobbly knee. He feared he would impair her performance, that she would be thrown, angry, offended by his presence. That she would somehow disgrace herself before the students. (How few there were! Why so few? That made no sense.) Vanessa looked down at her notes, made a mark or two with her pen, and raised her eyes for the first time. And remarkably, she saw her father in the back row of the small lecture room, looked directly at him, exchanged a glance, and smiled, with transparent happiness and confidence. She was not daunted, she was not awkward, she was not angry; she was simply thrilled that he had bothered to come, thrilled as adults rarely are or can rarely admit to.

She stood calmly in front of her audience, and spoke with gentle authority, squinting a little in concentration, her usual manner, explaining that this was the first lecture of the term, that it would be introductory in nature and that she hoped the students wouldn't be too distracted by her pine-green cast—"a recent tussle with the stairs, which the stairs apparently won. Not the color I would have chosen if I'd been sober—no, no, that was a *joke*— but for those of you keen to explore the philosophy of color, and fascinating philosophical questions like whether such a property as 'green' actually exists outside your perception of it—you still have time to sign up for Professor Isaacson's highly recommended class on David Hume. As long as you realize that it can't possibly be as good as *this* class." She continued: her class would focus on the history of ethics, pretty much from the greats to now, from Aristotle to Adam Phillips, with a double emphasis on philosophy as action and philosophy as reflection. There would be a guest lecture at the end of the semester, by the British psychotherapist Adam Phillips, attendance at which was mandatory. Yes, that's how we can pay him the big bucks, she joked.

"*What does the philosophy major prepare you for? Life!* Some of you will recognize that: I'm quoting from our department's own website. Is this true? Does philosophy prepare you for life? Well, you could say that if philosophy means anything, it means a discipline—in both senses of the word—that is at once abstract and practical, theoretical and concrete, intellectual and moral, affective and effective, a way of thinking that would ideally negotiate a modus vivendi between *reflecting* on life and *living* life." She referred her audience to some words on the handout, words she had reproduced from one of the course's required texts, by Bernard Williams: "the only serious enterprise is living, and we have to live after the reflection; moreover (though the distinction of theory and practice encourages us to forget it) we have to live during it as well." The only serious enterprise, she reminded her audience, is *not* philosophy—"Williams perhaps suggests that if we had to, we could do without philosophy. Because the *only* serious enterprise is living. That we can't do without. Yet to be alive properly, fully, is also to reflect on being alive, to think about life. Which is one definition of doing philosophy: so we come full circle. *Thinking about life and living life.* What is the difference? Is there a difference? Can we choose? Another wise philosopher, a teacher of mine at Princeton who herself had three children—she was always running hither and thither, always late for everything

and super-busy and harried—once said to me that if you want
plenty of time and freedom to *think* about life, then don't have
any kids. It goes without saying that hardly any of the great philosophers did. But, my wise friend continued, if you want to actually *be* alive, then you should have children and enjoy having
children. Which will make you a better philosopher—so she said.
Williams, by the way, had three children." His "very eloquent
passage," said Vanessa, would act as a kind of motto for the entire
semester.

Alan's nervousness had quickly disappeared, as if he'd taken
an aspirin: his impressive daughter was in easy control of her
small audience, bringing up quotations and names and dates
with what seemed to him magical authority; pausing occasionally to make a joke; turning at one moment to write "Categorical
Imperative" on the blackboard. Kant's famous law will come up
often, and whenever it does, she said, "I'll just refer to it as 'C.I.'—
it isn't a forensic detective show on TV." (Some laughs from the
keener students.) Lulled, weary, proud (she was different in front
of the students, and how attractive Van seemed, too, in her smart
"teaching clothes"), he got sleepy, and had to use his old driving
trick—sharply nipping his right earlobe with his nails—to stay
alert. Now she was talking about Aristotle and *eudaimonia*, "sometimes translated as *happiness* or *well-being*, but perhaps best
captured as *human flourishing*." Aristotle, Socrates, Kant, Adam
Smith, Nietzsche, Freud, Simone Weil, Bernard Williams, Peter
Singer . . . Alan's mind drifted from the subject, but not from
the subject of Vanessa. Though your child was only briefly a child,
you never quite got used to seeing her no longer one: there she
was—how strange—a formidable grown-up. Wasn't adulthood,
really, a fantastical and frail thing? And it was unbearable that
this confident, appealing, intelligent, authoritative woman was
the same person described by Jerry Dent—just a sad child again,
weeping like a child in church, the pain "coming out of her," lying
at the bottom of her stairs, "in pretty bad shape." If he described

that person, that failed adult, to the students, not one of them would believe him. Dr. Kunis would not believe him. He loved Vanessa with all his heart; and he detested the idea that he had ever loved her because he pitied her. Vanessa was always going to have everything. The special first child. She was brilliant and fortunate from the moment she emerged into the world: the Nigerian midwife, the birth blood still on her dark hands, lifted tiny, red Vanessa up, then laid her on Cathy's breast, and said, in her beautiful accent, words he never forgot: "It's a girl, and a very *lucky* girl—only the *best* for her. Only the *best* for her."

33

Dinner that night was unexpectedly easy. Alan had skipped lunch with Vanessa—after the lecture, she was busy with students and suggested that they eat quickly, with Dr. Kunis, at the campus café, an atrociously Van-like notion—and had set out again in the Toyota, to do some sightseeing. In the evening, he reported on his "findings." Sitting at the pine table, Josh and Vanessa gently teased Alan. Perhaps because the subject was America and not England, he was breezy and genial, as proud of his ignorance as of his newfound knowledge. He would leave the news of Jerry's "intervention" to the next day.

Alan had got his lunch that day at Scooby Don't, a diner in town he selected because of its promising shabbiness, as you choose the second cheapest wine on the list. At Scooby Don't, he had something called a Hypocrite Burger (veggie burger with cheese and bacon)—one of the most delicious things he'd eaten in a long while.

"Yeah? Truly? I've never eaten there," said Josh.

"Nothing hypocritical about the flavor," said Alan. "But I have a question. What exactly is *American cheese?*"

"Okay—it's a fairly bland processed cheese, usually orange or yellow, that you, um, get in America," said Josh.

"American cheese is . . . American cheese," Van said, laughing.

Alan had experienced another moment that involved the word *American*. After lunch, coming out of the diner, he almost tripped over a small dog, whose owner had stopped to light her cigarette. Even though he didn't like the dwarfish mongrel at his feet, but because he'd almost killed the damn thing, he reflexively praised it. What kind of dog is that? he politely asked. "What kind?" A small pause. "Oh—it's American," she had replied.

"The thing is, I couldn't tell whether she was joking or not," said Alan.

Almost in unison, Josh and Van assured him that the owner was joking. Americans *do* have a sense of humor, you know, added Vanessa.

"I'm getting the hang of it," said Alan.

"There's a lot to get the hang of," said Vanessa, "and some of it's quite weird. I still can't stand all the American flags everywhere. That's the mark of my foreignness, I suppose."

"What cracks me up," said Josh, "is these massive stars and stripes flying outside totally ordinary buildings, like Toyota car dealerships and McDonald's, like the country is collectively shouting: *this* is what we're proudest of. At least in Chicago they hang from some actually cool modern buildings."

Alan was really struck, for the first time in his visit, by Josh's physical appeal: his interesting, handsome eyes were shining; he was full of vigor and quick intelligence. His lisp evaporated when he wasn't nervous. Also, how much younger than Van he seemed: Vanessa spoke pretty much like her dad, while Josh sounded—well, young and American.

She was cheerful tonight: her first class of the semester had gone well; Dad had seen her at work. And Helen had left. She missed her, she always missed her sister when they were apart. Helen was as close to her—that terrifying line about Allah—as her jugular vein. But it was an awful truth that Helen's absence made everything easier simply because her presence made everything more difficult. Helen was taking a BA night flight from JFK, she would be in the air by now, laying her business-class seat flat over the Atlantic . . .

And Josh was gentle tonight, keen to leave a good final impression, perhaps because he was going tomorrow for a two-day trip to Boston—a big assignment, interviews with a couple of computer scientists at MIT—and now it wasn't clear that he would see Alan again, before his departure for London.

The trip to Boston caused the only moment of disturbance. Vanessa had thought Josh was away only for a day; she was clearly disappointed by news of the extra night. Not just disappointed, thought Alan, looking carefully at her, but almost fearful—a gleam of disquiet, of need, crossed her features. She quizzed Josh. Where was he staying? When precisely was he coming back? Nowhere fancy, said Josh defensively, just the Holiday Inn in Somerville. "Back almost *exactly* forty-eight hours later. I told you about this two weeks ago."

"Then you *won't* quite miss Dad, actually."

She insisted that he had never mentioned the two nights, only the one, but of course he should take as long as he required. The sound of permission hung in the air for a second, until Vanessa caught it, and herself.

"Wish we could come with you," she said lightly, "but I've got my other class tomorrow, and Dad has another appointment at Scooby Don't."

34

Alan woke around 3:00 a.m., with no idea of where he was. This had occurred once or twice before in hotel rooms, but always resolved itself quickly: like a computer screen going from "sleep" to active. In the stifling bedroom in the Alexandria Hotel, he seemed to be unable to summon his past, as if some terrible amnesia of the night had rubbed him out. Where am I? He turned on the light, but the room was completely unfamiliar to him. Have I had a stroke? All right then, I know what "a stroke" is, so I have language. But where have I come from, who am I? He climbed out of bed and stumbled to the desk. I can move, perhaps I haven't had a stroke. Where am I? The room stared back. His fear was rising, and to control it, he looked down at the desk, and saw a pad of paper, with "Alexandria Hotel, Saratoga Springs, N.Y." printed on it. He could feel these words moving around in his head, slowly, like huge pieces of furniture. So slowly! And then, in an instant, everything was restored to him—yes, I have come from Northumberland, I am in Saratoga Springs to see Vanessa, Helen had come, too. And by definition and extension, I am Alan, son of George (deceased) and Jenny Querry (still alive), former husband of Cathy Pearsall (divorced and deceased), partner of Candace Lee, father of Vanessa and Helen. He felt suddenly very sick, and spent a minute hanging over the bathroom sink. The nausea passed, and when

it did he sat on the cold lavatory bowl—he'd left the seat up—
and wept with gratitude and shameful fear.

Of course, in the morning, with dry American light as solid
as truth on the other side of the window and the smell of hotel
bacon drifting under the bedroom door, he had no fear, only un-
ease and puzzlement. Was it some kind of seizure? He felt perfectly fit. What was really unpleasant about the incident was that
it reminded him of something that had occurred a couple of
years ago, which he had privately named "the Hadrian's Wall
moment." It was late July. He had decided, on an afternoon whim,
to drive to Housesteads, and take Otter for a walk along Hadrian's
Wall. The air was soft and mild, the grass springy. Cow parsley
made milky fringes on either side of the road. He parked the car
and started walking with the dog. There was a high point, which
he reached after twenty minutes, from which you could see the
great wall stretch over the undulating landscape, for miles and
miles—an immense Roman fortification, an achievement of
Empire, the northern limit of Europe, as far as the Romans were
concerned. But also appealingly native: the local stones looked
like any other drystone wall in the area, only bigger. As far as the
eye could see, the great wall prolonged itself into the far distance,
all the way to the sunlit horizon, where it disappeared into wide
vagueness. It was beautiful. And then suddenly, as quickly as a
sudden wind, it was frightening, too: the wall seemed to stretch
all the way into the vagueness of death. That was the only way
he could think of it. He was looking at a ribbon of life, at the ribbon of his life, and he was looking at the end of life; and far
away, in that wide, diffusely sunlit, invisible horizon, was all of
death and all the dead, past and future—his grandparents, Cathy,
his father, his mother (all too soon), Van and Helen (sure enough,
in time). And himself? Sure enough, in time. He felt dizzy, and
sat down on the damp grass. Where the wall ended, *there* was
death, waiting. It was not, he thought afterward, a religious insight.
It was older than religion—the certainty of extinction, the shortness

of life. Over there, where the light thinned into infinity, over there it awaited him. For two thousand years, the wall had stood guard over the futility of human endeavor. No, that wasn't quite right, he thought now, because in fact the wall spoke not of the futility of human projects but of their longevity. You could build something, something grand, that would silently chaperone generations of people through the futility of *their* smaller existences. *The thing well made, that our children's children may be beholden to us.*

He would never forget that awful sensation of falling, of falling into history, into the long history of death. Without looking again at the horizon, almost shivering in the warm, blessed air, he walked back to his car.

He never told anyone about it, and he hadn't visited Hadrian's Wall since then.

35

Not feeling like breakfasting on his own, a little shaken by his nighttime amnesia, he phoned Vanessa and took a cab to her house. He wanted a repeat performance of the morning before (minus Jerry the evangelical missionary)—he wanted the experience of sitting at Van's table, drinking coffee and reading the paper, while she pottered around upstairs like a schoolgirl, getting ready for the day. Josh was leaving that morning for Boston, so with luck he might already have gone. Then he intended to take the Toyota and drive to Troy. And then maybe to Malta: he wanted to see the "famous" church that Van had visited with the Dents, the one that advertised its Sunday bread-making skills.

To his disappointment, it was the other way around. Van was almost on her way out the door—early meeting with a student—and Josh was sitting at the breakfast table. Alan begged Van to watch her step—the arm! It was a little warmer than yesterday. Sun doused the kitchen; the sky was very blue again, "American blue" was how he now thought of it.

Today, Josh seemed keen to linger in the kitchen. They were alone.

"You're leaving soon?" he asked. Yes, he was picking his rental car up in half an hour, said Josh. It was a trek: a cab had to take him a mile or two up Route 9 to the Hertz office. They talked briefly, meaninglessly, about how Saratoga Springs had grown, and Alan expressed surprise about all the restaurants and cafés on Broadway: there must be ten at least. Someday, said Josh, the main streets of all the richer American cities will have become one continuous, giant restaurant. "It's all anyone does or cares about, now. Eating out." Alan nodded, and was about to open *The New York Times* when Josh surprised him by sitting down opposite him at the pine table. His glossy young eyes gazed at Alan's tired face. He was willing himself, daring himself, to say something.

"Alan, you're sitting here, in America, because I told Helen about problems Vanessa was having. So basically, you're here because I asked you to come."

"Well, Josh, I'm here because I care about Vanessa, and I want to see her life in Saratoga Springs. And with you," he added.

Josh made a gesture with his hand, to flick this away.

"Yeah, of course. What I mean is, since you're partly here because of what I said to Helen about Vanessa, then you deserve to hear from me about—what's been going on."

The boy seemed nervous, but he didn't look away.

"I would be very grateful."

Josh told the story of how they met (at the conference in Boston), how he had been living in Somerville, sharing a small damp space with a housemate, an old friend of his from graduate school, a guy he had thought he liked until he turned into a total control freak—and was really happy to come to live with Vanessa in Saratoga Springs. They read books together (of course, straight off, Van gave him a massive, "totally untenable" philosophical reading list), and they discussed ideas like adolescents, way into the night, and laughed at the same bad TV shows; they bought a new bed (Alan took this to be Josh's discreet way of saying that they had sex, maybe even good sex; he wondered, for an uneasy second, if Van had ever *had* much, before Josh).

"But happiness," Josh said, "doesn't come easily to Vanessa. For some people, maybe for someone like me, happiness is like all the other things you take for granted—inner-ear balance, say, or the regular thump of my heart, or my ability to sleep at night. Not for Vanessa. It's like she doesn't have that inner-ear balance. You and I walk down the street and don't fall down; for her, falling down is kind of like the default position. *Not* falling down is an achievement for her, something she has to work at. But you know all this already—I didn't. And if I sound like an instant expert," he added, "it's not just because I live with Van. My youngest brother, Neil, has been dealing with stuff like this since . . . forever, it feels like."

"You're right about Vanessa," said Alan, clenching his hands, "but I just don't know why, I don't know *why*."

"Well—"

"Yes, all right, I know *why*: in the same way that I know why I have less money this month than last month: because I spent too much. But I don't know *why* I got myself into the weak position of spending too much and having less money this month than last. Does that make sense?"

"Alan, it's really not about weakness."

"I didn't mean it to sound . . . look, Van and Helen went through so much. Cathy and I divorced—that was exceptionally hard for the girls. Of course it was. It was a bitter divorce, and I had to soldier along on my own, not always doing as good a job as a father as I thought I was doing. Van and Helen took sides; Van blamed me, I suppose."

"When did Van's mother die?" asked Josh, though he knew the answer.

"Eleven, no, twelve years ago: 1995. Cathy's death was . . . we don't speak about it much—never, now. And their dad has a new girlfriend. Who is younger than him. I understand all that. But still: look at Helen, for goodness sake! Unhappiness isn't inevitable by any means. It still doesn't really make sense. Why one daughter and not the other?"

"Well, unhappiness isn't inevitable, but then neither is happiness. My brother has far less cause than Vanessa, but he's finding it a real struggle right now just to get out of his goddamn bed, and spends most of his waking hours smoking weed. I think he'd smoke weed in his *sleep* if he could. And our mom is a psychiatrist . . . So—I don't know if it's helpful to think about *why*. It should be *how* and *what* and *if*, not why."

Alan was stung by Josh's "far less cause," and resented that Van was being yoked together with the pot-smoking deadbeat brother. But he was touched by his gentleness, his attention and sympathy, his intelligence. He remembered Van saying to him, as they walked in the icy twilight—how long ago *that* seemed now—just before the glorious klaxon horn of the train, that Josh was the kindest, most decent person he would ever meet. That train, that train . . .

"Van doesn't much like being alone, you know," said Josh.

Alan thought, ruefully: *since meeting you* she doesn't much like being alone, because she's in love with you and wants to be sure of your love. Before she knew you, she spent many content hours on her own: in her bedroom in Northumberland, lying diagonally on her bed, reading those enormous philosophical books.

"Sometimes we fight about this. She gets anxious about me staying out at night for a drink, or taking an extra day if I'm away in New York, or wherever: You heard her last night? . . . Well, everything really changed one evening at dinner, about three months ago, when she asked how I would feel about moving to England with her. She's bored with Saratoga. I get it, so am I. It's why I need to get away. But I don't know how I feel about England. How would I work there? I don't know anyone in Great Britain. We're a tight-knit family, Neil and I are really close. So I guess I hesitated, and Van—I think—took my hesitation to mean I won't really commit to her. She didn't exactly say this, in so many words, but . . . Alan, you've *no idea* how fast she began to go down. I was really frightened. Her eyes—on bad days they were just *dead*, something just died behind them. I really did what I could, I *insisted* she go to a doctor, not just to the therapist. And ultimately I contacted Helen, of course."

"It was really bad?" said Alan. He wanted to blame Josh.

"Sometimes it was like she didn't inhabit the words she was speaking. I can't quite describe it. She was hollowed out. As if, when she spoke, she was doing a kind of ironic voice-over to her own life. God knows how she managed to keep on teaching at the end of last semester."

"Were you frightened that she would try to do herself harm? Was that what made you fearful?"

"Rightly or wrongly, I was frightened, yes. That's why I wrote to Helen."

"But look—did she throw herself down those stairs? Even if she did, it's hardly a suicidal gesture, is it? I mean, you couldn't *kill* yourself that way. There aren't enough stairs!" His voice had risen, his fists were clenched, and Josh looked at him with frank sympathy.

"I don't think she tried to kill herself, Alan. I think she needed to get someone's—my—attention. It worked. I couldn't take her depression, and I ran away: I went to my parents in Chicago. Not something I'm proud of. And then Van fell and broke her arm and of course I came back right away. We went back to Chicago together, and my parents *totally* loved her. They changed *my* sense of her."

"Of course they loved her."

"And since we came back, she's been better. Like winter and summer. It's funny, almost exactly the same moment I got in touch with Helen about visiting, Van began to get better. Like how your symptoms never actually manifest when you go to the doctor to complain about them? So you haven't seen her in anything *like* the state she was in six weeks ago."

"It was a kind thing, to take her to your parents for Christmas," said Alan quietly.

"Was it kind?" he asked, with some pain in his voice.

"What do you mean?"

There was a silence. A dirty minivan came up the clear white drive.

"It's very hard to live with someone's absolute *need*. I just . . . I don't *know* if I can be responsible for her happiness."

"Why not?" Alan asked, with more desperation than he intended.

"It's like someone saying to you: 'This is a very expensive vase, on no account must you break it.' Eventually you'll break it just *because* you were warned not to. I can't be responsible for her happiness, precisely because there'll come a time when I'm responsible for her unhappiness."

Ah, that would be one definition of love, thought Alan, but he merely muttered, with growing emptiness in his stomach, "I understand, I suppose."

They were quiet.

"Alan, if she really wants to go back to England, I don't think I can go with her. Not right now."

"Well then, she can just stay here, can't she? Both of you can just stay *here*."

Josh didn't reply, but looked at Alan with his expressive, guilty eyes, and Alan looked away, and his face fell, though he tried to hide it. He saw it: whether Josh knew this consciously or not, Alan had been brought over from England to look after Vanessa, in the event of the dissolution of her relationship with Josh. In fact, he had been brought over from England to manage that dissolution. Alan said nothing, merely shook his head from side to side as he looked down at the brimming newspaper.

"You see, maybe it *wasn't* so kind of me to take her to meet my parents?" said Josh. "With all the implications . . ." Again, he spoke in pain.

"Your instincts were kind," repeated Alan, the sadness slightly clogging his tongue.

The cab blared twice, quickly.

"You need to go now. That's your cab."

36

When the taxi had gone, Alan stood at the chilly window, looking out, as if the cure of whiteness would empty his head—the hard, packed drive, the white snowy roofs of two clapboard houses nearby, offered up like tilted blank canvases ... He admired Josh, suddenly—their conversation had altered his estimation of the young man. It couldn't have been easy to speak in the way he did. Josh still loved Vanessa. But he could not live with her. He was fearful, he felt Vanessa's unhappiness like a threat. Or he didn't love her *enough*, and could not live with her *enough*. One or the other, or a bit of everything—these were just different fractions of withdrawal. The withdrawal was the sum. Not this week or next, maybe not even this month or next, but sooner rather than later, especially if Vanessa was set on returning to Britain. Sooner rather than later, Josh would go. Helen had been right about him, though not perhaps for the reasons she offered. Maybe it wasn't fair to assume that Josh had asked Alan to come from Northumberland to manage the breakup of the relationship. Josh, he now noticed, had in fact asked for nothing, for no help of any kind. But Alan understood his new task. An idea began to form. Was he brave enough to carry it out? Could he say what needed to be said? Could he be as brave as Josh had been?

He wanted to talk—not to Candace right now, but to Helen. He went to the living room and dialed Helen's mobile in London.

"Dad! What's up? Is everything okay? How's Van?"

"She's out, teaching. I went to her class yesterday, sat in. She was very impressive indeed. Wonderful actually."

"Why wouldn't she be? She knows that stuff up and down, backwards and forwards."

"Yes she does."

"And Josh? Be kind to him, he's just a big excitable puppy . . . So what's up?"

"Josh has just gone to Boston for a couple of days. He's researching some long article."

"Again? To be completely honest, I don't like the sound of *that*. He's away an awful lot. What does he get up to, on these trips of his? I mean, if I were Vanessa, I'd keep an eye on him."

"No, no," said Alan sadly. "I think you're wrong. I think he's very loyal actually."

"What's happened, Dad?" she asked with suspicion. Alan was about to tell her, but suddenly could not.

"Nothing, all's well . . ."

She was getting distracted by something, he could tell.

"Dad, when you're back here—you come back in two days, is that right?—I *will* take you up on your idea. I'd like to bring the twins to Northumberland for a weekend, soon."

"And Tom, too, of course?"

"Yeah, sure. Tom, too."

"We'll make a plan."

"It was *fun*, you know, being in Saratoga Springs with you and Van, even if you didn't always feel that way."

"Oh, I did. I loved our train journey . . ."

"Me too—me *too*. I'd better go, someone's buzzing me."

"Off you go. Speak soon."

•

He set off again in the despised Prius. He was heading for Troy, but all he really wanted to do was drive and drive—through the cold suspended countryside, where the snow made everything equal. He would drive all day if need be. And at the end of his journey, having been to Troy and come back, perhaps all the old facts would be magically different.

He couldn't protect his daughters, he couldn't help them. Helen was a survivor, of course. Tough Helen could look after herself. But could Vanessa? In the lecture room, she had been so confident and easy, bringing up all her quotes and references. Alan was proud of her, as if she'd won the top prize at school. How much of that confidence and happiness now rested on Josh? Without Josh, would she quickly fall, as if a plinth were removed from a statue? And then what? How far would she fall? Josh *had* tried to withdraw—Alan knew this now—and Van had fallen hard. For some reason, he thought of how very differently each child used to sleep, and wondered if it was still the same. Helen used to lie in a kind of fury, on her side usually, with her knees drawn up and her arms tightly flung around her chest. She breathed through her open mouth, and frowned. Vanessa was peaceful. She slept on her back, and her features were serene and smoothed of worry. Distant, patient, calm. She seemed very far from life, as if in a Victorian photograph. He didn't mind waking Helen, because it would likely be a blessing. But Vanessa appeared to have attained a peace that waking would shatter. He would put his hand on Van's soft brow and quietly whisper—far too quietly to wake her—"Van, love, it's time. Time to get up. I'm sorry to do this . . ." He longed for her to find the peace by day that she seemed to have found at night.

He was driving past a modern church—a redbrick community center with a white witch's hat for a steeple—and then, only half a minute later, past another church, this one older and much more handsome, its dignity somewhat vitiated by a large banner that had these words: 1 CROSS, 3 NAILS, 4 GIVEN. More churches than bars in this state. In England, any decent village functioned on a two-to-one ratio of pubs to churches. He pulled up behind a yellow school bus, whose octagonal STOP sign was extended on a mechanical arm. The gunshot of American commands; he liked that. The blunt YIELD on all the signs that, at home, would have said GIVE WAY. He could *hear* that YIELD. If it was necessary to stop, then nothing worked better than STOP. Children were boarding the bus, dressed like schoolkids everywhere—like paratroopers or marines, bulkily padded and hooded, burdened by massive backpacks, huge plastic water bottles dangling from their belts like army-issue desert canteens. Ready for combat, the poor things.

Troy was half an hour down the interstate. He understood what Helen meant when she called it "Soviet." The snowy distances, the tall buildings and freezing, martial spaces; the big river, embalmed in ice, and lashed by a sternly unattractive bridge. Maybe Kiev or Ryazan was like this. The city had an overwhelming atmosphere of broken utility: empty warehouses, ruined factories by the river, many unused offices. People—Trojans, would that be?—moved through the streets as quickly as they could. Life was bitten down to the quick here, the cold punishing all civic life. But there were fine church steeples, beautiful old flat-roofed buildings, wide sidewalks. Gracious unmolested streets, apparently unchanged from the 1880s. Down by the windy river, it was an utter wasteland: weeds, rubble, grit in the eyes. But what an opportunity for redevelopment—there must be half a mile at least of empty waterside space, just waiting for the right hotels, restaurants, and flats. Build, and the people will come. Oh yes, like his beloved Dobson Arts Café. Troy should be twinned with Newcastle: the inhabitants would understand each other much quicker than a Geordie could explain himself to a Londoner.

Down a side street, he found a quiet bar, sunk in wooden gloom. But the barman was large-bellied, generous, very talkative.

He exuded an indiscriminate masculine joy. The regulars, as they arrived, were welcomed, and awarded equal banter.

"You behavin', Mike?"

"No."

"Ha!"

He told Alan to sit up at the bar, flourished a place mat, menu, napkin, and cutlery; Alan felt nicely babied, as if he were on a plane, in first class. His host quickly found out where he was from, and flattered him with counter-information.

"I'm figuring that 'coals to Newcastle' means your city has quite a lot to do with coal?"

"Coal, steel, shipbuilding. Used to. Newcastle was the first city in the world to have electric street lighting. Most of it has gone now. What we have instead are a set of splendid bridges. Well, we do still have the streetlights."

"Ha—back in the nineteenth century this place was *the* city for steel. Second only to Pittsburgh. That's what we did: steel. For the whole country. After the steel moved out, then we did shirts, we did collars, buttons. 'Collar City' wasn't for nothing. We've got the Rensselaer Institute. We still have some of General Electric. Huge company. Speaking of electric lights, you know that it was Thomas Edison who founded General Electric?"

"I didn't." Amused, Alan felt he was up against an American version of himself.

"Yeah, *that* Edison. But have to say, it's been kind of downhill from the time of the great man. People leave here, they don't come back. And this used to be one of the wealthiest towns in America! The new mayor has all these plans, sure, but I'm tellin' you, you can't rebuild a whole city by getting a few artists to move up here from Brooklyn. Stupid. *Stu*pid."

On the way back from Troy, the interstate was crowded, the cars moving faster than he wanted to go, and the salt and slush stormed against his windshield, as if he were piloting a small boat. He saw an exit for Malta, and took it. Van, Josh . . . leave it, leave it. The road was pleasantly rural after the busy highway— snowy fields on either side, a massive wood just coming into view over the hill. It was getting darker: a stunted winter afternoon. Van's radio station—he assumed it was her usual choice—was playing *The Four Seasons*, which Alan disliked as cordially as everyone else in the world did. To keep his mind off the situation in Saratoga Springs, he tried to listen to the familiar music as if for the first time. He leaned over to turn up the volume, a tiny downward gesture, only the tiniest moment away from the road, but when he looked up again through the windshield, a parked car he had not seen was preparing to pull out right in front of him. Alan had it under control: to pass, he lightly dabbed the brakes, touched the horn, and swerved out into the middle of the road. Nothing was coming the other way; he glimpsed a white bass drum in the backseat of the car he was passing.

He did not have it under control.

The steering wheel twisted in his hands, and suddenly the Prius was skidding, almost gracefully, without effort, right across the road. He pressed the brakes again, hard this time, in panic now, and the steering wheel retaliated and spun the other way. The car was gliding, gliding fast, and there was absolutely noth- ing he could do until the skid was finished with him. He had enough time to realize that he wasn't going to die, to see that the oncoming lane was still empty of traffic, to be grateful for his seat belt, which had locked and was tightly bracing him. The Prius came to a stop at the far side of the road. The accident, such as it was, had taken a few seconds. He had turned himself com- pletely round—he was now facing in the direction he had been coming from.

The memory of that queasy impotent slide made him feel sick. Vivaldi sparkled on. He'd been lucky, the car was untouched.

A young man, bearded, wearing a baseball cap, got out of his car, also a Toyota, Alan noticed, and ran across the empty road. Alan opened his door.

"Jesus, you okay? I'm sorry! I wasn't actually pulling out."

Alan's legs were trembling, his breath short.

"It's okay. I'm okay, the car's fine. Actually, I looked down for a second, to deal with this . . . damn . . . music." He pushed the Vivaldi off. "And when I looked up, you were somehow right in front of me. My fault."

"You must've hit a patch of snow or ice or something. They don't salt the roads much around Malta. Look, this was totally my bad. By the way, I'm Ryan . . . Your accent—is British? Where are you heading?"

Ryan explained that he was going to Saratoga Springs, too. He was a musician—hence the drums. His band was playing tonight and tomorrow night at Café Filippo, just off Broadway. Blues, folk, country. If Alan came, he'd give him the best seat in the house and make sure he got free drinks all night, too. Least he could do.

37

He drove back to Vanessa's house slowly—gingerly, as if he'd been burnt. She was home, thank goodness. He told her he'd been involved in a minor skid, nothing very much; Englishly, she offered him a cup of tea. He felt vulnerable, breached. Defeated. Van would look after him. He knew suddenly that he didn't want to spend another night in his hotel room. Absolutely not. He was no James Bond, not even a General Burgoyne . . .

She asked about Troy.

"I bet it reminded you of Newcastle."

"Yes, that's right. Amazing similarities. Good lord, that waterfront? Fantastic amount of empty land. Just waiting. The problem for Troy will be population decline. That's very different from Newcastle, of course, which is still growing." He was thinking aloud.

"Ah, Daddy, incorrigible . . . Maybe you should move *here*. So you had lunch in Troy? No Hypocrite Burger today?"

They sat at the table and drank their tea and talked about everything but Josh. About Skidmore and Van's colleagues, about Helen and Tom (Alan said nothing about the apparent marital difficulties), and Helen's new career (Van was full of admiration for her sister's resolve), and the old house in Northumberland, which held so much. Van asked about her grandmother, and Alan told her he'd been over to see Mam in the Home, just before embarking on the American trip. He didn't mention his anxieties about paying his mother's expensive bills, or the question he kept turning in his mind—whether he should ask Mam to live with him in the big house. Troy, which reminded him so much of old Newcastle, had for the same reason reminded him of his old mother. They did not mention Candace. They talked about Cathy, but by long-unspoken agreement, Cathy only entered family conversation alive, never dead. It was always "Remember when Mummy drove the Volvo into the ditch," as if she might conceivably drive the Volvo into the ditch again, or "Your mum and I went regularly to that hotel for a while," as if the termination was their decision and not one made by divorce and death. He looked at Vanessa's dear, known features— seemingly a little plainer and drier today, as if Josh's presence had been some kind of sustaining, revivifying drug. No, he was seeing too much in everything, thinking too much. She looked just the same, maybe a bit tired after a day of teaching, the same except for her spectacles, which she'd put on because her eyes were tired and her new contacts bothering her. The spectacles restored her to him: "old Vanessa." How he loved her blue, short-sighted eyes, her frown or squint of concentration, the tongue that slightly appeared when she became intense, her quiet voice and her soft, sidelong self-assertion. Even her complaints! How characteristic of Vanessa to moan that she missed Helen but was also glad she had gone, because "I struggle to get a word in edge-ways when she's around. Helen does manage to occupy the space around her quite tyrannically, you know." Alan had planned to have *the conversation* this evening, but he felt unprepared, he was still shaken. He would wait until tomorrow. For now, he would fall into the deep embrace of familiarity; he would rest.

"So—what questions do you have from *today's* adventuring? God, you made Josh laugh last night."

"Nothing comes to mind . . . No, I do have one question,"

said Alan, smiling. "When all these Americans, usually complete strangers, say, with apparently significant meaning, 'How are you?' are you actually supposed to tell them how you feel?"

"Not really. The best response is to reply with your own, slightly more intense, 'How are *you*?' at more or less exactly the same moment, so the two ideally cancel each other out."

"That's what I thought."

"Omelet and toast okay for dinner tonight?"

"Couldn't be better."

And later, after dinner:

"Van, would you mind much if I moved out of the Alexandria tonight and stayed in your guest bedroom? I've only got two nights left anyway."

"Of course not, I'd love it. I'm on my own. Why? Is the hotel getting you down? It would get *me* down."

"It makes me think of that old phrase 'fancy goods.' From my childhood—certain shops full of silly objects that no one wanted. They used to advertise 'fancy goods.'"

"I'd hardly ever set foot in that place until you visited. So— let's go and get your things. I'll come along for the ride."

38

He didn't see Vanessa the next morning; drowsy in bed, he heard her in the kitchen, then she was running up and down the stairs. He waited to hear the front door close, but missed it; woke again to silence. He'd just dreamed of Cathy. She was driving the old Fiat 500, and little Vanessa and Helen were standing on the backseat, as they used to, poking their heads out of the big sunroof. Then the scene shifted, in the way of dreams, and Cathy was no longer with him, and just before he woke he was, oddly enough, buying shoes for his daughters . . .

He had the sense of rising temperature; water was dripping from the icy window frames, and he had been woken in the very early morning by a carpet of snow sliding off the roof and falling deeply somewhere below. It was warm under the sheets. Ah, he had a pulsing erection. Old morning friend.

She returned for an early lunch, and they ate soup and toast, and Alan had the feeling he'd had the night before, of being almost a child again, with Vanessa as his sibling. What if the two of them just lived like this for days on end? It was intensely precious. Why not?

They sat at the table with their tea. He was about to speak, then hesitated; he didn't know how to proceed. There was a silence; Vanessa looked at him. He found a way in.

"I never told you, by the way, a strange thing happened. On Monday morning your Christian neighbor came round, when I was on my own, and tried to pray with me."

"What, Jerry? With you?"

"He held my hand, right here at this table, and we bowed our heads."

"Goodness," said Vanessa, "he's never tried anything like that on me." She stood up, started taking plates to the sink.

"Maybe not, but I think you're his real target, not me."

"What's that mean?"

"Van, it was Jerry who found you at the bottom of the stairs. He said you were in pretty bad shape. His words precisely."

"Of course I was, I had just broken my arm in two places. I was lying in snow! That's being *in pretty bad shape*."

"He also told me about you going to his church . . . and crying in church? 'Spiritual despair' is what he called it. That's also *being in pretty bad shape*, no? You're much cleverer than I am, so you must be pretending not to see what I'm saying."

"Dad, don't worry so, I'm better now than I was. Much happier. You can see that. Jerry found me at a very low point, for sure . . . But Helen said yesterday morning she'd never seen me as cheerful."

"When you were younger, Mummy and I used to worry about you so much. And now I'm worrying again."

"Too much."

"No, not too much. Not too much. You ran away! And those poems you wrote? And it frightened the life out of us when you decided you would give away everything you owned to your friends. Everything, even your precious books. Do you remember *that*? At Oxford? The university had to inform us about it."

"That was a *long* time ago. You didn't need to be so frightened. I know what you were afraid of. I've never been inclined *that way*, Dad . . . I was young, I thought I was being 'philosophical.' That's all it was, very pretentious indeed. Not as dramatic or morbid as you think."

"Van, tell me the truth. You didn't deliberately throw your-self down those stairs, did you? *Please* tell me the truth."

She turned, the tap still running, and moved to his side.

"It was an accident, Dad. Was it Josh who gave you the idea that I tried to do myself harm?"

"Yes, initially. He was frightened."

"I didn't know he had written to you with such . . . alarmism. I thought he just suggested that you might come and 'raise my spirits.' Look, Josh and I were having some difficulties, not get-ting on at all, and after an argument about possibly moving to England he . . . went away and he left me on my own, and I col-lapsed a bit. Some of the old awful stuff came back. I was very depressed, I will admit it. And yes, he was frightened, so he ran away. He knows he did the wrong thing. But after that fall on the stairs, Josh came back and asked me to go with him to Chicago."

"You liked his parents . . ."

"Yes, I met his family there—that was the real turning point. I loved them! I felt completely embraced by them. I know why he took me to meet them, because everything was different after Chicago . . . It feels like a new start. Josh said a few days ago that he might come this summer with me to England, to look around. An exploratory visit, see how we might feel about living there."

"You never told me you were thinking of coming back—to stay. For good, I mean. Helen filled me in on that. You know I'd love it. Absolutely love it. The tap's still running, by the way."

"We'll see . . . I admire the school here, I like my colleagues. But in the last year or so I've found I miss the strangest things from home—double yellow lines, BBC news at six o'clock, those weirdly small white radiators we have. Silly things like that . . . English birds!"

"*English* birds? As opposed to American ones?"

"Yes," she said defiantly, "English birds . . . and maybe Europe more generally . . . There's a Kantstrasse right in the middle of Berlin—that kind of thing I miss, you know? A street named after a philosopher! And I don't really have any close friends here, no one other than Josh. Thank goodness for him. Aristotle says that friendship is the thing human beings can least afford to be without."

"What if Josh doesn't want to come with you to England?"

"I think he does want to. And if not, we'll stay here."

"All right. Good. I'm glad." He paused, he was winded by the earnest, hopeful certainty of her reply, and could only press on feebly, without much attack. Strategically, was he going forward or backward? He *couldn't speak,* he couldn't speak a word of what Josh had hinted at the day before. It would flay her.

"Anyway," he weakly mused, "there was life before Josh, so there could certainly be life after him."

"Yes, Dad, there was, but it wasn't always very happy life, was it?"

"You are fine, ultimately. You just said so yourself."

"I wasn't *that* fine. For me, it's not so easy to be *fine.*" She sat down next to him and looked out the window. He followed her glance, over the waste white. Her eyes glistened. He could see the contact lenses, spectral, seeming to float. Her breath was slightly metallic. "I sometimes think I see too well, that's my problem, I see the bones of life, the structure of it all, that's my problem. I think too much."

"What on earth do you mean?" He tried to conceal his annoyance.

"I don't *want* to. I'm doing Nietzsche with the students later in the term, and he says that we should learn to forget, that we should become skilled at *not* knowing. He says that we envy the animal, and want to ask it, 'Why do you just look at me instead of talking to me about your easygoing happiness?' If it could, the animal would reply: 'Because I always immediately forget what I wanted to say.' It's fine pagan wisdom, but not wisdom I've been able to act on."

"Ah, Van, all these years, whenever we've talked about any-thing serious you've offered me a reading list."

"You see that house there? The one on the right. You see it has a screened porch? In the summer, my aged neighbor sits there. Professor Ensor. He's a wonderful fellow, genial and very cheer-ful, walks everywhere with a little camouflage-pattern backpack and a stick, ninety years old, still living alone. Belgian, originally. A retired medievalist—he taught at Skidmore forever. Before going into academia he was a monk, but he fell in love and left the Dominican order and got married. Later, he lost his Christian faith—for rather a wonderful reason. It was around the time they announced the Hubble space telescope and all the amazing things it could see. He suddenly realized that if the great thinkers he studies and reveres, all the people from the Middle Ages, Aquinas, Duns Scotus, Dante, and the rest, were to hear about the new telescope, they would all want to gather round it, to look into it and up to the spheres of heaven, up to Paradise—to see God, and Jesus sitting on God's right hand, and all the company of angels, and I don't know what else. In his mind's eye he could *see* these men excitedly, expectantly gathered round this telescope. He explained all this to me one day. As soon as Ensor thought *that* thought, he realized that he wasn't a believer; he realized that he would have had to disappoint those great think-ers and inform them that there's nothing up there."

"Very interesting indeed, but let's get back—"

"I'm not finished, that's *not* the point of my story."

"Okay."

"In the summer and fall, he sits in that porch and reads, and often takes his meals there. And last September, I saw him eating his lunch. He was alone, he's mostly always alone except for a not very friendly middle-aged daughter who occasionally visits. His wife died about ten years ago. So: I watched him while he ate his soup. It took ten minutes, and it was oddly hypnotic. He sat at a flimsy card table, hunched over the bowl. His hand slowly, patiently, methodically moved to the bowl and then up to his mouth, again and again, back and forth, taking very slow mouthfuls, until he was finished. Then he picked up the bowl and put it to his mouth, and drained the remainder. It was like watching exercise. I admired this monkish patience—he has great discipline, great fortitude—and I was also horrified by it. There was no discernible pleasure in the meal, just the discipline of *going on.* Of continuance. The reflexes of longevity. He was simply feeding a body, so that it could continue. For what? Well, to continue living alone for a little longer, so that he can *eat more soup* . . . It seemed an absolute image of life: the utterly meaningless, repetitive continuance. That's what I mean by seeing things too well."

"But . . . you said yourself—he's very cheerful. He still walks everywhere. So it *can't* be an absolute image of life." Why did she think like this, in these massive terms? He was desperate to keep things prosaic, local. "And maybe," he added, "it was the best soup he'd ever had in his life? You don't know how much pleasure it brought him. It sounds pretty meaningful to *me.*"

"You should be one of my students. Yes, he *is* cheerful—he's an absolute model of sane, fulfilled cheerfulness. He has made his life just as meaningful as it needs to be."

"But not a model you can easily follow."

"Not easily. Not without effort. That's what it means to be an adult, for me. And when there's effort, when you are concentrating so *hard* just in order to be alive, it's not really good cheer, is it? Not exactly 'human flourishing,' is it? Dad, you said when we walked along the road, you said you weren't 'naturally buoyant.' Those were your words? But I don't think that's true. You were humoring me. I think for you it *is* natural. It's innate. Is happiness just a trick of birth, a completely accidental blessing, like having perfect pitch? Josh has it: healthy, instinctive optimism. Helen has it, mostly. I don't have it. Do you ever *think* about it?"

"About being happy . . . I don't think about it really. I think about many other things, for sure, too many other things, but not about whether to be happy. Happiness, since you're asking, seems more like . . . a desire or stabilizing energy or force—"

"—and less like a puzzle."

"Not a puzzle, no."

Alan's resistance had turned to sadness. He cleared his throat and took his daughter's hand.

"You said that the professor, your neighbor, has 'fortitude.' My love, fortitude is important. You told me a story, so can I tell you one? When I was at school—many centuries ago now—there was a nasty bully called Welby. He was always going around the school yard trying to give boys a fat lip, trying to start a fight. Instead of fighting him, which was what the big bastard clearly wanted, we clever lads—there were only three of us in that lousy school—used to taunt him when he came our way: Welby, why do you want to start a fight with your fists? What's wrong with words? *Are you no good at swearing?* And that worked. We were immune. He turned away. Sometimes what I wish for you is that you could just swear at life rather than always getting into a fight with it."

"I think I know what you mean, but I don't know how to apply it to me," said Vanessa.

"I don't know either, quite. I wish I did." He tried again. "I mean—outwit life, tell it where to go, tell life just to sod off, and do it with . . . defiance. Close it off—the problem, I mean. Just don't *engage* with it so much. Don't let it get so big. Does that make any sense? You go to war with the army you have—I suppose that's what I mean."

"Rumsfeld?"

"He wasn't wrong about that."

They smiled gently at each other; he still held her hand. He gripped it harder.

"You know how precious you are to me," he said.

"I do know it."

"Mummy loved you so much . . ."

The past tense—he hadn't meant to use it. She made a small sound in her mouth.

"We had a family," said Vanessa, wiping her cheek, "and it was the best one in the world, and then it stopped being the same family and it all disappeared forever."

He could never bear it when the children cried. Half in pain, half in anger, he would remonstrate with them; quite sternly but in actual anguish he would always say, "No, come on, stop it, there's really no need for that."

"Come on, Daddy," Vanessa said to him, "it's okay, it's going to be all right. Let me get you a tissue. One for me, too."

They sat quietly for some time. There was much more to say, much more, but now he had a feeling that there would be plenty of time to say it. If not today, then tomorrow.

39

He suggested going out—dinner at Café Filippo was his sly proposal. Vanessa would never have thought of it, but sure, why not? He told her he'd met a musician who would be playing there tonight. "You've met more people in the last two days than I have in eight years here," said Van, a joke which nonetheless pierced him. All day the snow had been melting, a wide thaw, so it was finally warm enough to walk into town. The air was damp. Filthy hard snow was still packed high against the walls of the shops, deeply impervious, locked there until the spring; but the quivering shop awnings were dripping melted water into his neck. Students in loud, loose, bleary groups shunted along the sidewalks, moving joyfully in and out of the warm coffee shops.

But it was quiet at Café Filippo. Alan was sorry that the band would have such a tiny audience. Presumably their fee was fixed and did not depend on numbers? It was pleasant there—wide wood floors, redbrick walls and a touchingly clumsy mural along one whole wall, which seemed to show a collection of musicians from the 1960s, playing together at an ideal party; he only recognized Joan Baez and Bob Dylan. The mural celebrated the fact that Baez and Dylan performed in this very café, said Van, before they were famous. A stage was set up at the front, with idle guitars propped against boxy amplifiers, and the white drum kit he had glimpsed in Ryan's car. They ordered dinner.

Around ten o'clock, as Alan was getting weary and thinking about leaving, the musicians climbed onstage. He was glad that he and Van were near the back, in the shadows; he never had any intention of taking up Ryan's suggestion of free drinks and a prominent seat. Now the room had filled up—those in the know did not come amateurishly early. Surely that was the Trask lady up at the bar? Wasn't it her? Van confirmed the identification. The band was introduced to the audience: Ryan on drums, Wes on bass (tall, long-armed, with spiky peroxided hair), Cat on the banjo (youngish, bespectacled, in her twenties), and Emmy on acoustic guitar (older, with a long silver-gray plait). They were called the Mystery Tramps, a name Alan thought quite terrible. Van agreed, but said that it was almost certainly taken from "Like a Rolling Stone," which perhaps mitigated the awfulness. Or increased it, whispered Alan, filling the role usually occupied by Helen. "How strange," whispered Van back, scanning his mind, "that we're here listening to music, without Helen!"

They played extremely well, far better than their name suggested they would, with precision and subtlety. Their second song was noisy and full of rage, and allowed the drummer to get busy: it was "one of our own compositions," called "When the Blues See Red." There were whoops and whistles from the loyal crowd. After it was over (Alan was mainly glad the noise had ceased), they took a moment to retune. To Alan, the process seemed unprofessionally slow. "It takes a village to tune a banjo!" joked the young woman. "We *tune* because we *care*," added the older woman. Alan was getting restless. The next song, said the older woman, "was made famous by Mississippi John Hurt, but was probably played for years, maybe decades, before he sang it, and no one knows who actually wrote the beautiful darn thing." It was called "Make Me a Pallet on Your Floor."

She began by playing an intricate series on her acoustic, picking the strings. The accompaniment was minimal—the bassist was barely touching his guitar, and the drummer was hitting only a tambourine and kicking his bass drum. It sounded cheerful, it was cracking along at a good pace, but the words were wintry, soulful. Alan was fascinated, and sat up, suddenly full of concentration. He had never heard this song, but he and his parents had loved "Hard Times Come Again No More," and one thing he'd always cherished about that tune was that it was a sad song, a lament, even a dirge, but with lyrics that hinted the other way, at resolution, solidarity, conviction.

> *'Tis the song, the sigh of the weary,*
> *Hard times, hard times, come again no more.*

That song had sometimes given him strength during his own hard times. It was neither purely sad nor happy, but had the wisdom of its mixtures; the fortifying power of dappled things. And it was the same with the song the band was now playing. "What is this?" he eagerly asked Van. "Shush, Daddy, I don't know, just listen." It was set in a winter landscape, there was a traveler, a bed for the night. He heard "Make me a pallet on your floor," and he heard "I'm going up the country by the cold sleet and snow." His eyes swam, he was even more grateful for the shadows.

> *Just make me down, make me down*
> *Make me a pallet down, soft and low*
> *Make me a pallet on your floor*

40

It was warmer still, next morning. Outside, water was trickling everywhere; the roofs of the houses were now bare of snow. He liked his little bedroom, its thin walls, the air coming in through the closed window. He had a single bed with a New England quilt. *Make me a pallet on your floor.* He opened his laptop and waited for the Internet connection. He wrote a message to Eric Ball. He reminded Eric that selling off the Seddon was the top priority of the next two weeks; after that, they would shift the two buildings in York. He gave him Vanessa's telephone number, and explained that he had quit the hotel. This was where he could now be reached. And he asked him to contact Helen, whose e-mail Eric already had, and set up a three-way meeting in the next month, in London or Newcastle or somewhere else, it didn't matter where. Eric, Alan, and Helen were going to get together to discuss a new venture. "Exciting, I think. (More to follow.)" Then he logged off, shut down the white contraption, and serenely bade it farewell.

Downstairs, he sat with his coffee and read *The New York Times*. Van was in the main room, reading for class, pen in hand. The phone rang, and it was Josh, so Alan stepped out the door onto the front deck. For the first time since his arrival, it was warm enough to do so without flinching. Van had said that when spring came, she could feel her body unclenching—you've gained another lease on life, she said, you've successfully finished another precarious chapter. He understood that. Spring was still far off, but now he could imagine it in this landscape: the plains of solid ice would turn scabby and piecemeal; the redundant snow, packed against the sides of the buildings, would weep away into the gutters, leaving grit and salt on the perilous sidewalks. Then would come the movement, the blessed stirring he knew so well from his old life in Northumberland—it was the season when he and Candace would start their long walks, and long before Candace, he and Cathy: the daffodils would come, and then the sharp yellow life-stab of the forsythia bushes, like an advance envoy from summer; and the frivolous, brief cherry trees; eventually all the birds would return, the swallows and cuckoos, and the male chickadee whose hopeful minor third, a mating call, she would hear every morning at the bedroom window. And upstate, upstate, spring would turn to summer, with peals of wisteria bells, and the strong trees—the poplars, the maples, and the oaks— would fill out and become joyful green worlds again. Upstate. And the rest of life, that American life that had become Vanessa's world, would wake up, too. She would learn to love again the most familiar things: the crimson-and-black livery of the Boar's Head trucks (the triumphant gold animal, joyfully licking its lips), the growl of the brown UPS vans, the squeal of the rusty squat blue mailboxes (which looked, to English eyes, so much like rubbish bins), yes even the hard flap of the fifteen American flags on Broadway. The beautiful train horn would yell across the valley's warmed air—no longer the sound of a wintry Christmas harmonica, but now the searching cry of a migrant animal . . .

Van appeared at the door.

"Josh has to stay another night in Boston. Apparently one of the MIT scientists rescheduled on him at the last minute. So you *will* miss him after all. He sends his apologies."

He looked at her. She seemed untroubled by this news; but it was hard to tell. He knew what to do.

"Van, what if I stayed here a bit longer? Changed my ticket?"

"A bit longer? I'd absolutely love that, Dad. But how long?"

"I don't know yet. A little while."

"Well, well! You'll need some new clothes."

Boston, June 2017